COME ONE COME ALL

A TEN EROTIC SHORT STORY COMPILATION

MARILYNN HARPER

CONTENTS

CHAPTER ONE

INCUBUS

PART ONE

The last moments of flickering light danced across Daiya's freshly bruised face, a bruise given to her by the fist of her husband. Carefully dabbing the fresh droplets of blood with a wet cloth, she closed her eyes in heartache for all she'd endured and lost. The sting from his fist radiated down her cheekbone and across her neck, outlined by tears rolling scornfully down her face. Fantasies of leaving him dominated her thoughts, however, knowing very well what it would take to pull off such a feat wasn't a luxury she had been bestowed with. Mustering the sheer will it would take to carry out such a rebellious act was, unfortunately, repressed by years of self-doubt and low recognition of self-worth. Having been confined to the restraints of marriage at a young age, which certainly didn't help matters of confidence, to a man she had never met was a cultural business transaction. Therefore, leaving the arrangement was nearly impossible. Not to mention, incredibly risky.

Not only were these types of traditions held firm in her culture, but the few women who managed to flee ended up either dying on the streets, being killed, or being sold into the sex trade once caught. That was of course, after being raped and beaten by their husbands, and whatever groups they happened to be traveling the streets with.

She winced as the stained cloth soaked up whatever was left of his latest assault and tossed it into the basin behind her. It was eleven in the evening and her husband had been asleep for nearly an hour. He had passed out shortly after giving Daiya her nightly beating due to him being more intoxicated than usual. She was just thankful he hadn't forced himself on her tonight. She hobbled over to the bed. An unfortunate handicap she now lived with after he had laid his hands on her for miscarrying their only viable pregnancy. Being thrown down the stairs during her second trimester for not preparing dinner in time, the bleeding shortly followed.

Daiya's soul was no longer with her. Withstanding such levels of maltreatment, she often found herself dreaming of dying. She remembered the day her parents told her she'd been called upon as a bride at the age of fourteen. It was a monumental occasion as it had been said she'd never honor their family due to her skin tone. Being lighter than her siblings, she remembered her mother often being beaten over suspicion of her having an affair with a traveling American. Which, she adamantly swore never happened. To this day, she still didn't know the truth, and sadly, her mother passed away, taking her secrets with her.

There he laid, drunk on the one pillow they had. His snores killed any silence the night offered. She slithered under the sheet, careful not to wake him, and laid on her side facing the wall. Sleeping anywhere, other than by his side, was not advised or allowed. Her body was to be accessible during the night or the morning.

One last tear escaped through Daiya's lashes. It descended toward the bed before being absorbed by the old mattress below her as she chanted one wish. The same wish she prayed for night after night. And that was, to wake up from this nightmare and be in a place where she could be free. Free to breathe clean air, free to come and go as she pleased, and free from his touch. She had thoughts of ending her own life while he was gone during the day but could never bring herself to do it as it would bring great shame upon her remaining siblings and family.

Little did she realize that making such a sorrow-filled and desperate wish on this day in particular, that it would be granted. The day Incubus lurked through the remnants of people's crumbled desires and aspirations. The one day a year he was allowed to roam free, seeking meticulously the one he would conquer and devour. Listening, as thousands of pleas from above engulfed him, along with the agonizing cries from his captives, he waited for that one voice. One voice that would numb his burnt and hardened flesh and ignite his hunger for life.

Blood and water dripped down the stone walls surrounding him, turning to steam as it neared the ground of his cavern. Nestled conveniently beneath Satan's dominion, the ghastly creature patiently waited for his call. Being the Gate Watcher for souls who've tried, and failed, to escape the grips of hell, was a duty he took very seriously. Failure to contain these hellions would result in his immediate termination, which would land him right back in Satan's command with no chance of ever leaving again. He coiled his massive body atop the Looking Stone, dangling his tail above the head's of his soul toys. Listening to the screams of those embedded with pure evil and little regret, he reigned over them with his unique sense of torture. However mundane, a demon needed to feed after all, and being allowed this gift of pleasure was the only thing powerful enough to entertain him and keep him at his post. Having unbridled desires and no above-ground allowance, he accepted his fate here in order for the ability to have this one night. Otherwise, he'd still be amongst the riffraff above, riddled with a never-ending curse of turmoil. The salary of the Watcher was a prize many souls had fought for when presented to them by the Devil himself. Those who had failed to beat the unbridled strength of Incubus.

A role only to be filled by male demons and being allowed to rejoin the living for the most hypnotic drug known to men, made winning the only option for him. Having little memory of the person he was before death, one thing was for certain, he craved the essence of the female body. Craved it like the parched mouth of a man dying in the desert yearns for water. The way it flowed through his withered veins like warm silk, replenishing them with its addictive energy and force, was a prize he would fight eternal damnation for.

A flicker in the chaos of despair cycling through his hypnotic state caught his attention. And there it was. A single tear appeared on the top of his hand, unwavering despite the steam escaping from all around it as a result of his scalding flesh. This particular tear had traveled through realms in search of Incubus. A tear that would remain untouched, and unaffected, by the heat surrounding him until it led him directly to her. Incubus stood from his throne, a tall and ghastly creature covered in charred hair and scarred wounds. Raising his head, he lifted the arm holding the tiny droplet, a portal to the land of the living.

"Farewell for now, fiends," his body trembled and the piercing green of his eyes glowed with anticipation, "for my calling has arrived and therefore I must depart without delay."

He waved his other arm in a circular motion, conjuring the power of hell to corral those in squalor from escaping during his leave. An otherwise heinous retribution which, apart from this day, was only delivered for behavior that was less than desirable. He also found entertainment in it on a whim when his already devoid sanity quivered with madness and felt like playing. Their continued screams now softly echoed beneath their added confinement as Incubus reveled in this moment. Blood pulsed through his groin as he began to shift. Keeping most of his enormous size and embellishments intact, the remaining pieces of him transformed into a human replica. As the burning flesh of his nightmarish appearance turned a lighter shade of red, his swollen, black filled, veins shrunk and disappeared into his body. His flesh was smoothed, and his teeth dulled, so as to not leave fatal injuries, or scarring, on his cherished prize. In the altered state, Incubus would be allowed to fully relish in the pleasures of man, as he once had long ago.

Daiya's dreams were filled with rolling mountains covered in snow. A cool, crisp stream trickled down and spread freely into a private ravine where she basked in her solitude. Snow was a magical element of nature not seen in her part of the world, yet she craved the cold. A reprieve from the humidity and suffocation that encompassed her everyday existence. However, these moments of escape that tickled her imagination never lasted. They always turned into a horrific scene where the whiteness of the snow came flooding toward her, engulfing her in her own whimsical fantasies and catapulting her back into the hell she was a prisoner to.

The night ticked on, quiet and without event. The only sound to be heard was the faint, but jarring, noise of Daiya's husband's breathing. A rather abhorrent symphony she was forced to sleep through on a nightly basis. Something stirred by her feet, to which she wiggled them and rolled over. Still half asleep and covered in perspiration, she barely felt the prick delivered to her toe. A delicate stabbing coated with an elixir mimicking conscious death. The horrible visions in her mind were coated in red and flowed together as if being melted away, swaying her into an erotic trance and giving the illusion of rescue and paradise.

Her body was fluid, hovering above the nothingness below her as a pair of hands began trailing up each of her legs. Drugged on whatever was flowing through her veins, the sudden stimulation sent her spiraling into a frenzy of arousal. A feeling she'd never experienced before. When what felt like hundreds of greedy fingers tickling her inner thighs, the moisture between her legs increased. Coating her sensitive flesh with feminine liqueur. Writhing under the sheet and taunting her sex, was Incubus. Completely and primitively enchanted with the bouquet he was manipulating out of her, he diligently persuaded on. His throat beckoned him to flick out his anomalously long tongue for just a sample, but Incubus liked the ache of temptation. His cock lengthened with each inhale he took as he licked his lips and continued to press against the barrier of her entrance with his infernal hands. Swallowing the abundant collection of saliva that had formed in his mouth and leaked from his lips onto the bed, he curled his beastly toes and rubbed his cheek against her leg. His nose inches from the fountain of feminine life he so desperately lusted after, the time for withholding was at an end.

Having this be his only chance before another three hundred and sixty-five days, having her be his choice, and having it finally happening had the tip of his cock nearly ready to explode. He knew his way around the female, and also knew how to reward her for her offerings, a dually equal pleasure-filled experience.

Feeling the ecstasy oscillating through the mortal female, derived by his doing, fed the longing he was plagued with every day that passed during his waiting period. The vitality women possess is unmatched and will forever be the single most intoxicating afterthought he'd take away with him as they'd haunt his memories.

He stretched his thick tongue toward her opening and slowly swirled it along the edge, savoring every ounce of her. Her legs bucked the moment her body felt him, a response he had envisioned and only increased Incubus' appetite. Reaching between his monstrous legs and wrapping one of his hands around his impatient dick before plunging into her with his tongue, he grabbed hold of her thigh and surrounded her growing nerve with his warm lips. Humming an anti-hymn into her, the inhuman strength of his melody had her entire body convulsing beneath him. She grasped into the air looking for something to hold on to, which only made Incubus more hungry. He tilted his head to lower his horns to which she clung to with her fingers and forcefully gyrated against his song. As her orgasm built, and the fluids dripped from her, the flavors she provided sent him spiraling. With great force he began jerking himself off to the rhythm of her movements. However, a stirring beside them ripped Incubus from his focus. Turning his head to see what was intruding on his play time, her entire body went limp the second he broke contact. Sedated and content.

When he noticed it was a man, he slowly rose from Daiya's body and out from under the sheet. Reluctantly releasing the tight grip he had on himself, a deep growl escaped from the pits of his fury. The man next to him shot up, terrified, and propped his arms behind him for support as he backed himself up against the wall. Moments away from his eyes bursting from his face. Incubus tilted his head and examined the man. He noticed a pillow where he slept, yet none for her. He then noticed the wound on her face, a face he had not yet gazed upon. This angered Incubus almost more than the need he felt to be inside this female. Turning back to face the trembling man, Incubus asked him a question.

"How did the flesh of this female get impaired?" His voice was strong and his tone fierce, waiting for the answer he already knew. The color of his eyes changing to a deep red as he watched the man try to speak. His mouth hung open in silence as if he was about to break out in song. "Can you not hear me, boy?"

The man stared, paralyzed in fear and seemingly moments from passing out. Incubus brought his face closer to him so their noses were inches apart. The man could smell his wife on the creature's heated lips.

"Did you mark this woman?" This would be his final question and he knew from the man's cowardly expression that there would be no answer. Flames of rage filled Incubus and without hesitation, he shoved one of his clawed hands into the man's chest, grabbing hold of his heart. The man gasped and his eyes rolled back in his head.

"You dare think your impish and cowardly hands have any right maiming the flesh of those who bring life?" Incubus snared his words, exposing his fangs while pulling the organ loose from within his body. Still attached by it's arteries and veins, her soon-to-be expired husband watched as the creature before him twisted the stringy hold it still claimed within his crumbling body until one by one each strand popped and coiled out of him. Death beckoned the man and as the life drained from his flesh, he turned to face his wife. Seeing her sleeping with a smile, he scoured his face. With Incubus' free hand, he clutched the man's jaw and turned his attention back onto him. A cough of blood spilled from his mouth and with one final look, Incubus said calmly, "I'll see you in hell. I encourage you to try your little games of power with me there, after I'm through showing your bride what the pleasures of the flesh is supposed to feel like." And without warning, Incubus yanked the heart free from his body.

11

The commotion went without notice to the female as her mind remained in bliss, suspended in a cool wrapping of dreamed up silk, eagerly awaiting her treatment to resume. She could still feel the tingle his exodus had left spreading underneath her skin as her body remained hovering on the edge of ecstasy. The lowered humidity surrounding her supplied her body with reprieve from her daily suffering and the protective cloak she could feel wrapped around her abated every bruise and hardship she had ever possessed.

Incubus finished the bloody snack he had stolen from the man and snapped his fingers, sending the corpse to Satan's feet. Licking himself clean, he watched her sleep. Daiya's curves called to him and her breathing was rapid. She was a vision of life, all that he has long been rid of. Her scent found his nose, turning his already inflamed eyes into a crazed look of wanting. His balls stirred with readiness. Slowly lowering his body directly over hers, his hands sinking into the mattress on either side of her still face, he toyed with her pussy using the head of his swollen dick. Squeezing only a modest fraction of his tip into her narrow gate, he lost his ability to breathe. The sensations were forceful and fierce, and it took every ounce of strength to keep from plowing himself inside of her. His size was beastly, even after being lessened during his transition, and entering her completely needed to be done carefully. Pain was coming, but too much would thwart her pleasure, which would defeat the entire intention. Taking heed and delivering only unheard of ecstasy would be, and will always be, the only way to ensure the maximum amount of allurement.

He seeped into her, the ridge surrounding the base of his head almost completely submerged. With one tender thrust, Incubus reached a point of no return. She grasped his arms when the magnitude of his size stretched her beyond her normal threshold. Luckily, Incubus was well equipped to handle such an intrusive penetration. Curling his body, he placed his warm lips around one of her breasts and began sucking gently while kneading her nipple with his tongue. Her legs flung around him and her body bucked as he continued to deliver his drug-filled saliva onto her hardened flesh. Pulling with suction in order to open her duct-ways, his fluids absorbed by them. Within minutes, her tightness softened and relaxed, allowing his enormous dick to slide in with a little more ease. She was ready, and subconsciously begging to be taken. A desire she had never dreamed of having.

She moved her hips side to side, rubbing her clit against his veiny cock as he slowly submerged himself into her. He opened his mouth to release her breast, allowing it to bounce to the side, and reached forward to grab hold of the headboard. Closing his eyes, he flexed his ass and plunged his entire length into her. Roaring into the air when his fertile stones collided with her asshole. Keeping full tilt, he fucked her slowly. Allowing himself the pleasure of feeling her walls twitch and clench around him. Keeping pressed against her clit, his humping coaxed as much of her juice out of her as it could. Leaving her gasping for air. Her entire body began to tremble and he knew she was about to come, giving him exactly what he had come for. Not wavering his pace, he lowered his head and stretched out his tongue until it reached her other nipple and coiled his snake-like tail up to her puckered back hole. Pushing the small bulbous tip of it delicately inside her asshole, he twirled and bobbed it to enhance her pleasure. The triple onslaught of attention pushed her over the edge and she shattered around him within seconds. Slapping and panting filled his ears, which only made him hammer inside of her more forcefully. She screamed. Daiya's body froze in a state of ecstasy, unable to handle the bliss exploding out of her.

Keeping himself at bay until every ounce of her penetrated his tight flesh. He could feel his body regain its vigor with every passing second. He cried out and rolled his head back as his entire body rapidly started to feel alive again. This was all it took for him to resume his force and retrieve the mortal fountain of life. His fingers cracked through the wood of the bed as he began slamming his fullness into her again. She wailed and clung to him as his curved dick pounded against her sensitive insides. From the size of him, she could barely breathe in her place of dreams, the slight pain only adding to her arousal. Keeping his tail snuggly in place, he started plunging it in and out of her to the same rhythm of his fucking. Eager to draw out that which he so coveted, and enough to keep him partly satisfied until next time.

His nuts trembled and collected with each powerful thrust as their bodies slapped together. Incubus released one of his hands from the headboard and wrapped it around her lower back, arching her body for the final moments of their union. Daiya's head bobbed and her eyes fluttered when he pressed her body tightly against his, keeping his momentum. Her walls squeezed his quivering cock as she neared her second release, causing his right leg to shake and his mouth to drool into the mattress. Banging her like a rabid beast, he growled and ripped half the bed apart, never wavering from his assault. He was barely in control and Incubus could hear her heart flutter as her entire body vibrated below him. Tilting his head up, the demon inside of him howled into the night as he poured himself into her. The heat from his cum sent electric shocks throughout her body and caused her to erupt with cyclone force. To which Incubus immediately removed himself from her and dove between her legs to lick and suck every offering she bestowed while she came. His eyes rolled back as he devoured her elixir, unsure if he'd be able to part from the sweet nectar. Pulling at her clit harder, the sensitive nerve continued to rattle between his lips. Burying his burning tongue deeper inside of her to reach the highest, sweeter juice, he grabbed both of her ass cheeks and pressed his face against her wetness. Rubbing side to side as her body oscillated in his hands.

Forcing her against his ravenous mouth, he drew out another orgasm. She grabbed onto his horns once again and bucked against his face until every single drop she had was taken, leaving her spent and completely fulfilled. When Daiya's body finally calmed, it started to shiver, which Incubus was familiar with. Panting, he rose to his feet and stood tall, having to hunch over in order to stand. He was massive, and he felt reborn. Watching Daiya sleep, his devilish eyes narrowed as he took one final glance at her swollen pussy. Licking his lips he grabbed hold of his massive cock and collected the rest of her dampness from it with his hand and licked the last of her off of his palm as he moaned with gratitude. Placing both of his hands together, he closed his eyes and began chanting an ancient hymn. Within seconds the air in the room started to spin, surrounding both of them.

When Daiya woke, she was no longer in her bed. She was no longer in her home. She was laying in front of a fire outside and surrounded by snow as white as the clouds. Unsure of whether or not she was dreaming, she looked around and saw a cottage behind her. Her legs were weak and her pussy was gloriously tender, having no recollection as to why. She simply felt amazing. Making her way to the back of the tiny home, she slid open the door and smiled. She wasn't sure how long she'd be here, but finally, she felt free. Somehow, she knew this was her new home. And in the nights that followed, she dreamed of a beast touching her in ways no one else had, as her belly grew...she wondered...

To be continued....

CHAPTER TWO

THE RETURN OF INCUBUS

PART TWO

When the gates of Hell open for Incubus, once every 365 days, his exit bears the risk of carrying an unseen companion. Due to the intense heat and ground quaking accompaniment of the demon-guard's morphing, microscopic larva can drop from the walls of the damp catacombs and attach to the Incubus' transformed body. This 'spawn' migrates into the seed of the Incubus and holds firm until it's transferred into the host body of the female. During the time of breeding, it travels into the womb of the targeted and grows alongside the offspring until it's developed the ability to infest the fetus. There it will remain for the duration of its incubation. Taking a full year to fully mature and reach the strength needed to hatch, the spawn will then consume the host from the inside out and grow at rapid rates until it claws its way out of the child. Freeing a creature so heinous, it travels in the shadows and unleashes unspeakable terror onto anything it touches.

This is what happened during Incubus' last visit. Feeling the sting on his skin where the leech had clung to, he paced in front of his captives. His massive hooves smashed down on the steaming stone floor and his body trembled with anger. It had been almost a year since he'd last visited Earth and he remembered the female well. In fact, she above all others had stuck with him and consumed his mind. Knowing he'd never be able to find her again now that she was living in peace, there was something mysterious about her that he just couldn't shake. Her taste was the true nectar of life and her scent lingered throughout his memories like an addiction.

It wasn't until recently that Incubus felt the burn of the spawn's trail, most likely due to the fact that it was almost time for it to break way from its host. A host Incubus himself had created. The few times this has happened since the beginning of time, the creatures of hell didn't survive the travel to Earth due to the unimaginable speed and heat, but there had been one account that one had successfully transferred into the host. Long before Incubus' reign, his predecessor didn't trouble himself with the trivial life that would be lost but rather longed for his own day of freedom to return once again. Incubus had a decision to make, knowing he would have to sacrifice this year's feeding if he chooses to save the child. A decision based on a child he couldn't care less about, but an oath that was etched into his existence.

Incubus was faced with a torment foreign to him. One riddled with thirst, fury, protection, and promise. Knowing his offspring only had days left before the spawn consumed its tiny body, Incubus knew the only way to keep his woman at ease and in the place he had created for her was to return. And now, he had a beacon that would lead him there. The only trouble was, removing the creature without harming the child was not an easy feat. However, Incubus was prepared to sacrifice those parts of himself in order to honor his chosen one.

Cruel and ruthless, the spawn will immediately begin wreaking havoc the moment his flesh comes to light, which would include the woman Incubus had rescued. Little does the spawn know, the Incubus' wrath holds a power far greater and serves a purpose that never loses. Especially, with what he has to give up in order to come back.

...

Daiya closed her eyes and remembered the agony she experienced during the birth of her daughter. With no one else in sight, her screams echoed through the snow-capped mountains as she pushed through her contractions and delivered the most beautiful being she's ever laid eyes on. Being alone, she was forced to endure the onslaught of pain, with limited ability to rest and ease, as she tended to her newborn.

However, months later, Daiya and her daughter remained warm, healthy, and at peace in their hidden away cabin. Consumed with not knowing how she had ended up here, away from her former life, she often woke up in a panic that one day it would all be gone and she'd be sitting in front of her broken mirror dressing one of the many injuries given to her by her husband. Or worse, he'd find her here and harm them both.

Taking in a deep breath, she opened her eyes and looked down at her nursing baby, and smiled. If this was a dream, she was devoted to savoring every single moment of it. Naming her child, Daysha, which means 'gift from God', gave her a sense of comfort knowing she was thanking the one most likely responsible for such a treasure. Although, on multiple occasions, her dreams were filled with a being surrounded by darkness that both frightened her and gave her immense pleasure. And if that wasn't alarming enough, she felt a certain connection between it and the child sleeping beside her. She'd often wake up in a hot sweat, panting and feeling herself all over for signs of contact after being convinced it had been real.

She ran a finger over her daughter's tiny button nose and across her cheek to a scar she had been born with. Yet another mystery she couldn't figure out. Knowing wholeheartedly that nothing inside of her womb could have caused such a jagged mark, nor would the child's nails be strong enough to leave damage so permanent. Coming out screaming as most newborns do, she remembers the fluids of birth coating the baby's face and initially not noticing the injury. Healing quickly, and not seeming to cause any continuous pain, the only time Daiya thought about it was when she'd nurse and fall asleep in her arms. Not knowing what hurt her child left her feeling helpless and afraid, and she hoped her little one would grow without being haunted by the same perpetual wonder. However, she knew that was unlikely.

Lately, Daysha had become increasingly more irritable. What used to soothe the child no longer worked and Daiya was beginning to get concerned. She seemed to be in discomfort and no amount of care or time seemed to remedy the little one's pain.

Holding her baby close to her, she hugged and bounced up and down in the hopes of getting her to sleep. Rubbing her daughter's back, her fingers grazed over something she hadn't noticed earlier. A hard lump the size of a plum rose from the side of her belly. Her fingers trembled and she softly felt around it while the child screamed.

"Oh, my baby," panic riddled her voice, "what is this?"

Assuming it was a tumor of some kind, Daiya fell to her knees and prayed.

"Please," she closed her eyes and rested her palms on her daughter's stomach, "please, don't take my baby."

Tears rolled down her cheeks and for the first time since being here, Daiya wished she had someone to hold on to. With both of them now crying, she laid down with her baby and waited for a miracle. Knowing that if Daysha didn't eat from her soon, she wouldn't make it much longer.

...

Incubus turned his hand over when the familiar chill of a teardrop seeped through his flesh. It hadn't yet been a full year and he knew he still had a few days to go. Confused by the early calling, he looked up to the portal and noticed its gate was still intact. If he couldn't exit hell yet, the presence of a tear was surely an enigma. Not to mention his desire for anything, other than the issue at hand, was non-existent. Examining the droplet of sadness closely, he noticed something was very different with its color. Typically, the visual would be clear with a white cloudy haze, but now, the inner cyclone was red. That could mean only one thing, and that was that someone he had once saved was in despair once again.

"It's happening," Incubus whispered to himself. The condemned souls around him moaned and screamed loudly, as they did each time Incubus spoke.

His chest expanded to make room for his anger and frustration. Without the passage of the gate being opened, the only other way for him to leave was to expel most of his power to plow through the mantel of the Earth. This was not an easy feat to accomplish as it took heavy concentration to permeate enough of his essence to surround him with protection during the speed and thickness of the layers he'd have to pass through. Not to mention the consequences he'd have to face from Satan himself for leaving without rule.

But as the tear in his red hand quivered, he knew time was running out. Looking up at the only exit he'd ever known, he closed his eyes and conjured his powers to leave him and mold to his external body. Unable to change his appearance during such an endeavor, he made fists with both of his hands and waited for all the shrieks and cries around him where muted by his extracted force-field.

Taking in a breath large enough to sustain him during his ascension, the room around him shook violently. Rocks became dislodged and fell all around him and on to the prisoners, as the sand by his hooves danced around him...

"I'm coming..."

...

Sleep was no longer an option and Daiya could barely see straight due to her fatigue. Taking her daughter outside in the hopes of the cool evening air helping, she wrapped both of them in a thick blanket and sat against the deck's frame. As she prayed for help, the ground around her began to tremble. Slowly standing, she gripped the stair railing with one hand and backed up toward the house. The windows rattled and the trees seemed to be vibrating right before her eyes.

Assuming it was an earthquake, Daiya turned to get inside to safety but before she had her hand on the doorknob, the ground behind her split open. The sound was indescribable and she was paralyzed in terror, too afraid to turn back and look. With her almost one-year-old screaming even more now, she reluctantly turned her head toward the explosion behind her.

Almost dropping her child, her eyes froze and her heart hammered in her chest when she saw what had caused the monstrous sound. The beast from her dreams was standing directly in front of her home, standing about ten feet tall and with arms as massive as the largest gorilla. His skin was red like fire and he had horns that curved and beckoned to her. She'd had visions of holding on to them and the onslaught of memories and sensations that came over her brought her to her knees.

"Please," she begged, "do not harm us."

Incubus walked toward them, his colossal weight causing the earth beneath him to shake and crack. Unable to move, Daiya fell to her side and clung to her child as the most dominating being she'd ever seen came within inches of them. Intense heat radiated from his vein-protruding statuesque body and warmed the area around them. Shaking, tears streamed down her cheeks as her Daysha continued to scream.

"Let me see the child," the deep vibrations of his voice rattled her rib cage and made her heart thud with fear. Incubus held out his massive clawed hand and kneeled beside them, still towering over their smaller frames.

"Please," Daiya pleaded and squeezed her eyes shut so she would no longer see the magnitude of dominance in front of her, "she's not well. Take whatever you want, but please leave us be."

"It is not my intention to hurt the child, nor you," He spoke with sincerity to which she opened her eyes to study his face. "Now, please, let me. There isn't much time left."

As Daiya contemplated handing the only thing she's ever loved over to a beast that could easily crush them both within his grasp, the lump on Daysha's belly started to move. Crying, she kissed her daughter's tears.

"Can you help her?" She sobbed and looked over at Incubus.

"Yes," he brought his palm closer to her, and with a hesitant breath, she reluctantly placed her beautiful daughter into the hand of a demon. Taking his pinky nail, he gently pricked Daysha's heel and waited for the effects of his venom to lull her to sleep.

In that very moment, images of a beastly creature having his way with her and sending her into a state of physical and emotional bliss, came flooding into her vision.

"You," she whispered.

Once the baby was calm, he stood, leaving Daiya far below, and placed his other hand over Daysha's belly. Closing his eyes, he assessed the stage of the spawn. After a few seconds, Incubus reached up to one of his horns and grabbed hold of it. With the screams of the child echoing in the air, combined with the praying of Daiya, Incubus roared into the sky and snapped the large black antler off of his head.

A powerful wave of air exploded from him and he dropped to his knees, a coating of blue fluid dripped from the wound and onto his face. Placing the child on the grass in front of him, he used his horn and painted his hand and arm with the liquid seeping out of it until all traces of his red flesh were covered. Daiya watched intently, having no clue what was happening but feeling as though, whoever this thing was, he was going to try and help.

Incubus looked up at Daiya, "Do not be alarmed."

She didn't answer and watched as the red beast brought his claw down toward her daughter's stomach. Gasping, Daiya covered her mouth and could do nothing but let him try.

Blue light shot out from Daysha's skin as his nails and fingers disappeared within her little body. Daiya screamed into her hands and flung herself over to her baby to hold onto her head and whisper to her that everything was going to be alright. Only the child never moved and remained peacefully asleep while the beast worked on her.

"What's inside of her?" Her voice quivered.

It didn't take long before he retracted his hand and Daiya watched as he pulled out a transparent circular sac containing something red and lizard-like. She almost passed out when one of its claws tore through the pouch and Incubus crushed it within his hand. Green ooze and remnants of the sack dripped from between his fingers before he devoured it and licked his hand clean. Daiya grabbed Daysha into her arms to look over the exit wound, but to her shock, there was no evidence anything had left her body. And the lump was gone.

"What?" She whispered, looking down at her now smiling daughter. "How? Who are you?"

"I am the child's father," he stood before them, with his horn discarded on the grass beside them.

"That's impossible," she didn't want to believe that all those dreams she'd had were real.

"It is not," he stated matter-of-factly.

"You saved my baby," she had nothing to offer him. "What happens now?"

"Now," he dropped to his knees, making the ground quake, "I can not return."

"Return?"

"My horns send a beacon that opens the door back to my lair," he explained. "Without both, I am no longer able to access it."

"You sacrificed your life? For her?" Daiya looked down at Daysha.

"And you," his black eyes looked past her eyes and into her soul. Feeling her relax in his presence. Even while in his true form.

"What will happen to you?" She whispered.

"I will weaken, and eventually deteriorate until I am no longer in existence," he didn't sound afraid or remorseful. Incubus knew the cost of what needed to be done.

Daysha turned her head into her mother's breast and grabbed at the cloth covering her. Looking up at Incubus, she wasn't sure she wanted to nurse her child in front of him.

"Feed her," he insisted.

Afraid to not listen to him, she carefully turned Daysha so her nipple could find her little mouth without exposing too much of herself. Within seconds, her daughter latched on and pulled from her as if she'd gone days without eating. Relief washed over Daiya's face and the Incubus watched with fierce curiosity as a pooling of dampness saturated the rest of her shirt from her other nipple leaking. Being exhausted herself, Daiya didn't even notice and opened her eyes when she heard a soft growl coming from the beast's throat.

With Daysha completely passed out with only having fed from one side, she held her close to her body with gratitude. However, she realized her thanks needed to be given to the mystical being who just saved her child's life. Their child. She had many questions that had long remained unanswered and a strong sense of urgency to rectify that surged throughout her.

"I," she was nervous to speak, "I need to go put her down so she can sleep."

"Go," his voice was deeper and filled with a longing she recognized.

Leaving Incubus behind, she went into the small cabin and tucked Daysha into her cradle. Smiling down on her healthy daughter and knowing she was now safe, Daiya decided to return to the creature outside.

Slowly creaking the door open, she watched as the beast ran his hands through the grass and held his head low. His left horn was still oozing blue liquid and it looked as if he was meditating or pleading for something. Hearing her, he looked up, panting.

Feeling the sting of having a full breast on one side, she walked down toward him. No longer feeling in danger, but still nervous around something so unbelievably large. Standing in front of him, he lifted his torso and sat back on his heels to face her. A small cloth covering his midsection swayed in the breeze and Daiya was presented with a fleeting glimpse of what was between his legs.

Unfazed by her noticing, his breathing slowed, and his eyes lowered to her chest. Being captivated by her, as well as slowing dying, he hovered in a place wedged between the realization of his demise and the need to taste her on him again.

"Thank you," she breathed and waited for him to look at her and away from the ground. "How can I ever repay you?"

"There is no need," he grabbed a handful of grass in each of his hands, making fists. "I will soon be a memory and you and the child will not be harmed again."

"I have so many questions," she took a step closer to him, curious about what it felt like to touch his steaming red flesh and wanting to ease his displayed hopelessness. With a shaky hand, she reached for his knee and placed her palm on it. Heat radiated into her despite being surrounded by land and mountains covered in snow. Apart from where Incubus was, the cold ground covering quieted the world and all she could hear was the hammering of his heart within his chest.

His muscles twitched beneath her fingers and he placed his hand on top of hers to feel her move over him. She stopped breathing and fell into a trance of uncertain emotion for the thing that cured her child. She was instantly overcome with the need to kiss away his pain and suffering while his body succumbed to its fate.

"The questions you seek answers to will not satisfy the bewilderment you've trapped within yourself. There are things you aren't meant to understand." He spoke in scripture to her and it caused her chest to heave. His attention was captured by her taunting breasts. "You should go inside."

His body trembled.

"Why?"

"Because there are parts of you I desire, and once," he clenched his jaw and spoke through his fangs, "the fire fills my veins I...won't be able to control my thirst."

"What are you saying?" Having a small idea of what he was referring to, she was doubtful their two bodies could do anything about it.

"I'm saying the essence of life you create within you is the single most treasured thing I covet, and its power torments me." Incubus' upper lip twitched and he swallowed hard trying to refrain from pouncing on her. After everything she's endured in her life, the vow he had made after her last offering would not lend way to him claiming her a second time. It would go against his entire compass. Not to mention he lacked the ability to transform into a more appealing visual due to him now only having a single horn.

His words rattled her. The combination of his very visible need for her, the way he sacrificed things she'd never fully comprehend to save her child, and the fact she'd been living in a state of mild confusion since being here made her ability to think clearly almost nonexistent. The strength exuding from his god-sized body overshadowed his heinous features and had her primitive needs swirling.

Even with her past abuse and aversion to men, something about this mystical being who she suspected had saved her all those months ago and filled her dreams, had awakened an energy within her she wanted more of. It was intense and made her feel capable of anything, which was a feeling she'd never experienced before. The only thing she knew, and it was certain, was that she wanted to ease his pain. And whatever came from that, she'd welcome.

"I don't want to go inside," she spoke boldly, and she knew it. Her worth to this creature held her chin firm, as she was consumed by a feminine energy she'd been praying for her entire life. Going inside was no longer an option.

He looked up at her and the blackness in his eyes ignited, "Please."

She moved closer to him, not afraid. His claws dug into the ground and grabbed hold of the grass and soil as if to keep himself in place. Inches from being between his spread open legs, she lifted her hand to touch his damaged horn. Incubus lowered his body so she could reach, keeping his eyes locked on her body and all its curves.

Her fingers caressed the side of what remained. It was smooth as silk and its rich blackness hummed against her flesh as if it were hurting. She knew it caused him pain and for many reasons. As she let her thumb run through the blue blood seeping down its side, something warm pressed against her ankle. Closing her eyes, she knew it was his hand and allowed every sensation her body felt from his touch to feast upon her.

Incubus moved his hand up to her calf and wrapped his palm around it, using the grip to pull her closer to him. Being the size of roughly three men, her body was lost within his as the heat from his touch seductively traveled up the back of her leg.

Surrendering herself to Incubus' hold on her, she was no longer afraid. She relished in the way his hand hovered under the lower crest of her ass and sighed above his crouched frame. Her body swayed to the strumming of his fingers as they taunted their way between her thighs, holding with them the promise of unbridled pleasure. Tilting his head further down, he used the point of his remaining horn to lift her shirt from her body, watching hungrily when he realized she was completely naked underneath.

A deep rumble echoed within his chest and through his hand, which was as close to her clit as it could be without touching it, causing her to moan into the air. Looking up at her expression,

Incubus smirked at her bliss and licked his lips when the aroma of her milk reached his scenes. His tongue slithered out of his mouth and circled her areola. When her creamy elixir saturated his taste buds, a frenzy mushroomed inside of Incubus and he could no longer hold back his restraint.

Gripping on to her ass, as hard as he could without hurting her, Incubus took her nipple into his mouth and wrapped his arm around her. Clinging to her as if he would die if he let go, he took from her let-down while massaging her clit with his free hand. The heat coming from his body began to rise and his drinking became more manic. It felt good against her exposed skin being in a wintry climate and made her weak in the knees. When she had no more in her to feed him with, Incubus began to shake. Releasing his hold on her, he flung both of his hands to his head and roared into the air.

Suddenly petrified, Daiya couldn't do anything but watch after having his hands abruptly missing from her body. Unsure of what was going on, she reached out to his face but he fell back. Looking all over him for signs of injury, her eyes widened when her sights landed on his broken horn. She couldn't believe what she was seeing. The blue that had been oozing out of him retreated back into the base of the horn as it grew painstakingly slow for her to witness. Incubus ran his hands over it, seemingly in too much pain to actually realize what was happening, and continued to howl in agony.

"Shhhhhh," Daiya tried to soothe him but her hushed voice was no match for the magnitude of sound he was creating.

Standing before him, naked, she had no other choice but to wait until whatever was happening to him ceased. Caught between wanting to ease his pain and the throbbing he left growing between her legs, a tear escaped her and rolled down her cheek. The sound he was making caused everything around them to shake and she worried it would scare Daysha.

Almost the exact replica of the horn that remained, Daiya watched as its re-growth completed and the beast calmed. As quickly as it started, it was over. Incubus opened his eyes and released his hold on the sides of his head. Getting back onto his knees, he panted and looked back at her.

"Are you hurt?" He murmured.

"No," she breathed.

He reached forward and wiped the tear from her face and brought it to his lips before taking both of his hands and examining his new horn. "You did this."

"I'm not sure I did," she spoke softly, looking over his enormous body and secretly hoping he'd touch her again.

"I am," he brought both of his hands together and closed his eyes. Within seconds, he lessened in size, still towering over Daiya, and his skin changed hue until it resembled closer to that of a human. Still keeping his black antlers and muscled physique, Incubus was now a size that was manageable in order to avoid harming Daiya.

When the change was complete, he wasted no time. Standing, she watched in awe as he approached her. A walking, God-like creature, naked and full of powers she'd never be able to comprehend, donned a look of intense lust that she surprisingly welcomed. As Incubus got closer to her exposed body, his dick filled and pointed right at her. Unable to hide her stunned reaction to the size of it, his hand reached her chin and tilted her face up toward his.

With his mouth parted, exposing his black fangs, he lowered to his knees to ease the discomfort of her looking up so high. With their faces now right in front of one another, Incubus studied Daiya's features very carefully as if burning an imprint of it into his mind. His hold on her was gentle yet strong as he continued to move her head in different angles. Watching him look at her, her breathing became more erratic with anticipation. The intensity of his eyes made her heart pound and when he changed course in his examination, going lower, her knees weakened with need.

Knowing he was gazing upon her breasts with desire, she could barely stand still with the quivering of her pussy. She wanted him to touch her there. But instead, he brought his other hand up and ran the side of it seductively down the middle of her chest, caressing the left one and bringing his fingers together to form a circle around her nipple.

She moaned and his eyes darted back up to hers. "Do you enjoy my touch?" His voice was husky with a dark energy that peaked her forbidden desires.

"Yes," she inhaled deeply and her breasts rose under his hand.

"Mmmm, that's good to hear," his fangs glistened under his lips and she longed to touch one of them. "Because touching you is perhaps the only thing worth dying for."

His words melted her and she could no longer maintain her composure. Literally swooning, he caught her in his arm. Her nipples pointing right up to him, he continued to toy with their hardness while positioning his dick between the legs of her aroused body. With one knee on the ground and the other upright at a ninety-degree angle, she nestled comfortably in his embrace while he manipulated her body in order to spread her moisture over his shaft. Bringing her deeper and deeper into his seductive artistry.

She sighed with each movement he made, allowing Incubus to relish in the soft coolness the air had on her flesh against his heated coating. Blood relentlessly filled his cock and the warmth of it brought Daiya into a soporific state of stimulation. Rendering each desire within her to awaken and linger restlessly until his touch feathered over every one of them with attentive precision.

Taking the tip of his shaft, Incubus used his hand to hold it against her slippery clit so he could gently massage it. The effects of his meticulous awareness of her were so profound, Daiya was left unable to move. Falling into an ever euphoric place only two bodies completely entangled in one another could befall. Savoring every connection, every moment they've spent longing and wondering when and if it would ever come again, the two were surrounded by a cyclone of pure lust and hunger.

Incubus' fangs lengthened with every twitch her vulva made against him and he could no longer wait to have her on his tongue. Lifting her entire body with ease, he brought his face in between her legs and cradled her ass and upper back with his hands. Lifting her head to look down at him, she watched as his eye contact with her remained intact as his tongue slowly slithered past his fangs and directly inside of her. Her back arched when the thickness of it stretched her in all the right places. Hooking devilishly inside of her and teasing her spot. Her mouth dropped wide when his upper lip toyed with her clit and the blackness of his eyes shot deep into her soul. Unable to breathe, she made little noises into the air the deeper he went inside of her. Swirling and drinking all of her in, her legs dangled free and trembled beneath him.

"Give me what I came for," he murmured into her sweet flesh, tasting every drop she produced.

Moving her hips up and down against his face, her clit began to ricochet throughout her. Incubus inhaled her scent, causing his eyes to roll back into his head and his thirst to increase. Growling, he made a seal around her sex with his large, dark lips, and sucked every nerve and crevice of her into his mouth. Screaming, Daiya's arms flung around frantically searching for something to grab hold of until her hands made contact with his horns. Gripping them, memories of this happening before melted into her mind as he drove her closer to her release. Completely letting go of all control, she squeezed her fists tightly around his antlers as her orgasm aggressively approached.

Humming, Incubus nursed on her as if it was the nipple he had taken earlier. Increasing the speed of his song and the intensity of his suction, Daiya's entire body spasmed into unrestrained bliss. Pouring a year's worth of need into his greedy mouth, she wailed as Incubus continued drinking from her. Slowly lowering her to the ground he had thawed with his presence, he laid her on her back while keeping his lips tightly wrapped around her quivering folds until every twitch subsided and her muscles relaxed.

Panting, she opened her satisfied eyes to find Incubus' large body on all fours and halfway up her body. Looking down between them, her sights landed on his incredibly visible pulsating cock. Swallowing hard, one thing she knew for certain was that she wanted this beast inside of her. And she wanted it now.

"What are you?" She breathed as his beastly face hovered over hers.

"I am your guardian," he reached down between her legs, and using his fingers he spread open her lips to allow him in.

"Is that what I call you?" She could barely speak as her breasts heaved below the pounding in his chest. His powerful touch ignited flames within her as they moved together once again.

"Incubus," he grabbed hold of his dick with his other hand and brought it to her opening. She gasped when the thickness of it threatened to test her span. "Ahhhhh."

The connection of their parts, even slight, caused Incubus' heart to pause its beating in order to absorb every sensation it created. Being swollen to capacity, he dripped into her and tried to hold back from slamming into her without mannerly preparation.

"Oh my God," she gyrated her hips to coax more of him in.

"Do not bring him into this," he growled and coiled his tail, unraveling it so the tip of it plunged into her parted mouth. "Let this keep that tongue of yours busy."

She rolled it around in her mouth, taunting him by mimicking what she'd do to his dick. Unaware that he had similar nerves running up and down the length of it. Flexing his ass in order to try and regain some resemblance of control, Incubus couldn't help but take a moment to relish in the way her mouth fondled the sensitive tip within her juicy mouth.

Grunting and closing his eyes, he took a hand to his cock and began stroking it to the rhythm of her sucking. Watching him play with himself brought Daiya to a level of arousal she had never experienced before. Working him harder and more seductively, pushing him to the edge. His hand pumping was now manic until his eyes flung open and he looked down on her drooling mouth. Pulling himself slowly out of her plump lips and letting his tail float back behind him, he stalked his way on top of her. Keeping his weight supported on his arms and legs, his eyes blazed the darkness of his desire and reflected in hers.

Leaning down until his lips wrapped around one of her nipples, she screamed in ecstasy when he sucked and circled it with his tongue before pressing the head of his vein-laced cock onto her pussy. Her breathing was erratic and full of want. Letting her breast fall from his mouth, Incubus bared his weight onto his knees and used his hands to push both of her knees outward and to the ground, opening her up completely.

Looking down at her saturated entrance, he pulled her up onto his legs until he was able to slowly begin entering her. Making sure she was well lubricated by spreading their combined fluids around her pussy, he gradually buried himself inside of her. Keeping his thumb on her clit, making sure it remained wet and properly attended to, he bobbed his tip in and out of her. Grabbing her own breasts and pinching her nipples, Incubus' upper lip twitched at the site. Moving faster, his balls began to tighten as her walls squeezed around him.

"Deeper," she begged, swaying her hips side to side and getting what she needed from his touch.

Obeying her demands, without complaint, Incubus sunk further into her. Gripping her legs harder, he tried to keep himself from exploding too soon but the snug fit was hard to combat.

"Careful," he warned. "Let me do the moving."

She stilled and watched as his massive frame held on to her and flexed with each soft pump he delivered. When he was buried halfway and the curve of him connected with her g-spot, her eyes shot wide and she grabbed on to his wrists.

"I said be still," his words were labored and she could tell he was close.

She wanted to reward him for what he had done for her and her child, and being seconds away from her own release, she decided to ignore his orders. Biting her lower lip, Incubus gave a look of knowing as she began thrusting herself upward to suck more of him into her.

His fangs dripped down onto their union, giving her inflamed skin a tingling sensation. The feel of her completely engulfing him was enough to bring him to the edge, but not until she came again for him. Bringing his tail back around, he placed it directly on her throbbing nerve. Her eyes looked down at what was happening and when it started vibrating, she almost choked. Her eyes rolled back in her head and her entire body tensed as Incubus gyrated in all the right ways.

Picturing how they must have looked, his huge muscled body towering over hers, fucking her out in the open, Daiya exploded within seconds. Her pussy clamped down on Incubus' dick, making it almost impossible for him to move. Letting her ride out as much of her pleasure as he could by keeping his tail in place, a rush of blood shot up to his tip, thickening him and opening his hole. She yelled out in pleasure as fire shot from within his nuts and up his shaft until he filled her with the store of pent up celibacy he'd been inflicted with carrying all this time.

Shaking the remaining bliss out of him, Incubus looked down at Daiya. Her skin red with desire and contentment. Holding her in place with his cock deep inside her, he made a face that could be mistaken for a smile. Devilish and captivating, despite the sharp teeth and snake-like tongue. She squeezed his pulsing dick with her stretched walls and Incubus snarled, pushing himself deeper into her than he had before. Her mouth gaped open and he kept still until he was sure his seed nestled exactly where he wanted it to...

THE END

CHAPTER THREE

3SOME'S COMPANY

J oyce crashed through the door of her three-bedroom apartment, holding mounds of shopping bags. Her roommates, Greg and Sarah, wouldn't be home until later and she was excited to start wrapping their Christmas gifts. At first, she was skeptical about living with a guy, but having Sarah here lessened the awkwardness of it. Plus, two girls and one guy turned out to be a great combo. She dropped her bags by the couch and went into the kitchen. The holidays made her giddy and she couldn't wait to sip on some spiked eggnog and pop on a Christmas classic.

Sarah and Greg had invited her to join them at the local bar for the annual Festive Karaoke Night. Though it sounded fun, she'd much prefer staying at home with a stiff beverage, roaring fire, and a cozy, old-school movie playing in the background. Grabbing her favorite Christmas glass, she poured the creamy beverage to the halfway mark. Its thick consistency sent a sense of nostalgia through her veins. Adding a generous whiskey topper and a sprinkle of nutmeg, she smiled and wiggled her shoulders in excitement.

Bouncing back into the living room, she placed her drink on the mantle and got to work on the fire. As the kindling lit, she grabbed the remote and searched for her favorite holiday movie, A Christmas Story. Finding it within seconds, she hit 'select' and retrieved her drink before kneeling in front of the baby flames. Between the heat coming from the burning wood and the smell of pine and eggnog, she was suddenly overwhelmed with cheer. She took a hefty sip of her drink and turned to empty the bags of all the gifts she purchased and needed to wrap. Taking one more sip, she got to work with the opening tune of Deck the Halls and Jean Shepard's narration filling the room around her. Between the nostalgia of the movie and the extra booze she added to her drink, she was definitely feeling warm and fuzzy.

By the time the movie ended, Joyce had managed to wrap every single gift and placed them perfectly under the tree, all while under the heavy influence of whiskey. Feeling a bit dizzy, she plopped herself on the couch and pulled out her phone to scroll social media and play Mahjong before heading to bed. Halfway through her first game, a clambering of some sort, accompanied with child-like giggling, seeped through the front door. She remained seated, knowing it was Greg and Sarah returning home from the party.

Taking longer than usual to unlock the door, Joyce chuckled to herself when Greg started scolding Sarah on her key aim. To be fair, it was freezing outside, and he did have a severe aversion due to his precious, baby-like skin. His own words. Hearing his incessant explanations about the struggle of having his entire body hair-free was both hilarious and ridiculous. According to him, he gets colder than the general population because he lacks a layer of protection. Joyce, however, never wasted an opportunity to remind him that having it removed was his choice.

They barreled through the door like a couple of drunken high-schoolers. Joyce tossed her phone to the side and turned around to face them.

"How was it?" Even though Joyce was aware of her own level of drunkenness, it didn't take long for her to realize her friends weren't sober either. Their hushed chuckles and traipsing were enough to confirm this.

"Oh my God, Joy, it was so much fun," Sarah blurted, practically landing on top of her when she joined her on the couch. "I'm so glad to be home. This one wasn't behaving." She pointed her thumb behind her toward Greg.

Joyce turned her head to Greg, who was struggling to unzip his jacket. "Tell me, what did you do this time?"

"She's overreacting," he mumbled. "I was harmless."

"Well, I've heard that before," Joyce giggled. She knew her male roommate well. Once the booze entered the man's system, a women-obsessed trance took over his better judgment. "Well I'm surprised to see you guys home so early," Joyce handed Sarah the glass of water she had gotten for herself earlier. "I wasn't expecting you back for another few hours. He must have really gone all out with the 'innocent gestures'."

"I'd say," Sarah pointed behind her to Greg, who, by now, was flailing around and cursing under his breath at his inability to get out of his coat, "old horn dog over there couldn't keep his mitts off any female that walked by him."

"So, a typical night out," Joyce didn't see how that shocked Sarah, considering Greg's reputation was well known by most at this point.

"Not so much," she refuted, "because what's not typical was him walking around with a very visible hard-on."

"No!" Joyce immediately turned to see if he was still pitching a tent. To her disappointment, he was not and was completely unaware that the two were discussing his misconduct. And package.

"Oh yes," she rested her head on the back of the couch and handed the water back to Joyce, grazing her breasts in the process. Sarah said nothing. "I was 'asked' to take him home after some rigid as fuck couple had complained to the bar manager. So embarrassing."

They both laughed, even though if it was anyone other than Greg, they wouldn't find it so funny.

Joyce's right eyebrow rose when she spotted Sarah staring at the tree in a daze. "You good?"

"So good."

"You should go to bed girl," Joyce rubbed her friend's leg, waking her from her sudden passed out state.

"I should go to bed," she slurred and tried to stand, but quickly fell back onto the couch.

"Okay, okay," Joyce stood and offered her her hands, which she grabbed hold of. Pulling her friend up, she helped lead her to her bed. Once she had her tucked in, she returned to the living area to help Greg. "Okay, enough. Let me do it."

Greg lifted both hands into the air in surrender and let her. After freeing the wedged material from the zipper, she made quick work of getting it undone and off of him. Standing with his eyes closed, she was now very happy she had made the decision to stay home. Having to wake up early tomorrow, Joyce knew she'd feel like shit. She was already hoping the extra beverage she had earlier wouldn't come back to haunt her. Feeling like shit, while serving breakfast to a crowd of senior citizens, wasn't on her bucket list.

"Now go to bed while I clean up out here," she hung his jacket and as he walked forward, she grabbed her empty glass to bring into the kitchen, not paying attention to his direction. When she returned, she was happy to see that he had listened and was in his room. "Good. He listened, for once."

She turned off the tv and flicked off the lights. Feeling tired, she made her way to the bathroom to brush her teeth. Still having the holiday spirit coursing through her veins, she gargled away the remaining toothpaste and with a pep in her step, headed to her room. It was dark and warm, and immediately she began to feel sleepy. It was hard not to with how cozy it felt in there. Closing the door behind her, she kept the light off and used her phone to guide her to her bed. Once she reached the mattress' edge, she was confused to see the comforter all jumbled up. Certain she had made it this morning, as she does every morning.

Keeping her phone's light aimed at the scene, she moved it further up only to discover a head of sweaty hair on her freshly washed silk pillow. "What the hell, Greg."

He didn't respond.

"Greg," he showed no sign of awareness. She groaned when she realized he wasn't going anywhere. "Oh...fuck it."

She went to the other side of the bed and crawled in. It wasn't the first time he'd done this and she didn't have the energy to try harder to wake him. Plus, it wasn't a big deal. They'd been friends for years and she wasn't unfamiliar with this behavior. Although she would have preferred it if he hadn't chosen her side of the bed, as that was her favorite pillow.

She moved around until she got comfortable enough to fall asleep. It didn't take long for her eyes to get heavy. However, not more than two minutes later, her bedroom door slowly cracked open. Letting in the lights from the Christmas tree.

"Joyce?" Sarah's voice echoed into the darkness.

"What's wrong?" Joyce spoke over Greg's lifeless, snoring body.

"I'm super dizzy," she entered the room, leaving the door open behind her.

"Okay," Joyce didn't know what she wanted from her. Sarah fumbled toward the bed and clumsily felt up and down Greg's body before moving her way over to the other side of the bed.

"Why is he in here?" she whispered when close enough, her words melding together. "Move over."

"What?" Joyce scolded quietly. "There's no room. I'm failing to understand how my bed is supposed to help with your spins!"

But her words didn't reach Sarah's ears, apparently, as she flung back the sheets and crawled in next to her.

"Oh my God guys, really?" Joyce knew neither of them would answer her.

Now, being surrounded by two different variations of erratic breathing, Joyce laid on her back, her personal space critically imposed upon, with her eyes wide open. Regretting her decision to move in with two over-grown children, her eyes once again began to cooperate and lower. Sleep would be her only savior at this point. She contemplated moving to one of their rooms, but she hated their mattresses. Joyce had very particular tastes in comfort, after all.

With all of them snoozing pretty heavily, Greg, while deep in la la land, rolled over and covered half of Joyce's body with his left leg. This, of course, ended her trip to slumberland. She groaned and tried to free herself from the weight of him but was too restricted with Sarah attached to her like a magnet.

"Seriously!" she said out loud and immediately regretted it. On her thigh, she felt a very obvious erection beginning to form. "Okay, nope."

She tried one more time to break free, but lacked the will and gave up fairly quickly considering the more she moved, the more it seemed to affect him. A fact that currently, she wasn't sure she minded. Being almost two years since she'd been with a man, the feel of his firmness against her suddenly began to give her tingles in places she had almost forgotten about. As if it had a will of its own, most likely due to her being buzzed, her leg started to move a little against it. Feeling the hardness against her bare leg was rather exciting, and the fact he was passed out offered an unique opportunity. Not intending to go any further than what she was doing, those plans quickly went out the window when his body began to respond to her movements.

Her eyes popped open when he began to hump her in his sleep. At first it was gentle, subtle, but within no time at all, it progressed to a more pressured and incessant grind. Her clit twitched and she reached down to touch herself to relieve some of the need that had started to grow between her legs. When her fingers grazed the top of her underwear, Sarah's arm reached across Joyce and placed her hand directly on her breast. Joyce froze, her lips parted. Having never had a girl touch her, and knowing she too was asleep, she decided to go with it. Holding firm the intention of pretending tomorrow that it was all a dream.

She began massaging her growing nerve and between the motions of Greg and her own arm, she knew it wouldn't be long before she came. When she felt Sarah's hand tighten, Joyce was shocked at how it made her feel. A surge of electricity fired through her. Greg continued to press himself into her and the build-up was becoming too much for her. An idea came into her and she acted immediately on it, not having the will power to decide otherwise. She carefully tilted her body toward Greg, trying to position his cock between her legs. Sarah moved her hand from the left tit over to the right as it was now closer to her and continued to massage her nipple. The dual sources of stimulation was next level for her and she couldn't help but try and get off on his, now manic, cock. It was like being with a teenager, overly eager and inexperienced but yet thrilling none the less.

Greg fell right into place and continued thrusting himself into her sweet spot. It was as if he now knew where he was, even asleep, and became relentless. Joyce could feel her cheeks heating and her climax approaching as she laid motionless, letting them both use her body as a play toy. Her panties were soaked due to his animalistic rubbing, causing them to slide side to side with each thrust. She moved her hips slightly in order to lessen the tease building for a minute, otherwise she would erupt within seconds. But that plan would soon go out the window the moment she felt a different sensation against her skin. A feeling she knew well, despite it being years since she had last experienced it. The bare tip of his penis had escaped the hole in his boxers and grazed along her exposed lips each time the material shifted.

It became very clear and very obvious that if she kept going, at this rate, they'd soon be fucking. Unsure if that was something she was truly prepared to go through with, she tried to move in such a way that prevented him from entering her. But the feel of his shaft running itself up and down the lips of her pussy felt way too good for her to keep him out much longer. Her body began to tremble with need. Having Sarah's hands running up and down Joyce's stomach and over her breasts resulted in little fight to give, as the head of his cock was now adamantly struggling against her entrance.

She wanted to scream out in ecstasy but didn't want to wake them. She absolutely didn't want to wake them. Something about the sleeping attack had her more aroused than she had ever been. It was wrong, which made it that much more enjoyable. Sarah began moving her hips against Joyce's ass as Greg continued his unconscious efforts to enter her. The pleasure was indescribable and incredible. The three of them swayed together, humping and growing with explosive need. Knowing how badly he wanted to penetrate her made her even more wet and excited for what was to come.

Sarah grabbed hold of Joyce's hip bone and began rubbing her clit quicker against her as she subconsciously built herself into an erotic frenzy. Joyce could tell her friend was close, as was she, making her no longer able to resist being taken by him at this point. She tilted her pelvis to allow his eagerly searching dick to slide into her with a few effort-filled pumps. The size of him, as it slowly made its way deeper and deeper inside of her practically made her eyes pop out. Trying not to lose it right then and there, she was pleasantly surprised by his aim and almost exploded when he hit her g-spot on the first full thrust. Gearing herself for what he was about to deliver, she didn't anticipate what happened next. Reaching around her and gripped onto Sarah's back, he slammed himself into Joyce with the force of someone in dire need to fuck. The entire bed shook, causing Sarah to reach her orgasm and moan into Joyce's neck. It was becoming more difficult to hold off her own release. As Greg continued his pounding, squeezing his thickness into her, and the sensation of his warm, tight flesh moving in and out reminded her of the fact that she needed to get out more. Having waited this long for something this good was just dumb.

When Sarah's vibrations began to fade against Joyce's backside, the nerves under her skin began to spark and pop. Greg pressed himself hard against her, causing her to almost stop breathing due to the close pressure he had on her pulsing button. The way the entire scenario was playing out turned her on more than she'd ever imagine anything like this would, breathing was no longer a concern. She wrapped her arms around his body and allowed for a deeper pounding. The muscles in his ass clenched as he pushed himself further into her, slowing his thrusts before he erupted. Her tight walls welcomed his cock. Joyce was ready. Since he had slowed some, she took it upon herself to continue moving herself up and down him. Squeezing her muscles to coax the climax out of him and to offer more friction, he began to tremble and once again forcefully hammered into her. Sarah was now passed out cold behind them.

The aggressive force of him resulted in their bodies to roll back, leaving him on top of her. She wrapped her legs around his waist and they gyrated like rabbits until the tension was too much to handle. He grunted into her neck as his dick swelled and poured into her. He pumped out his release while squeezing both of her ass cheeks and mumbling words she couldn't comprehend. Her mouth flung open as every single nerve between her legs spiraled out of control around the throbbing of his cock.

Her clit grew with each pulse of pleasure it delivered. Their orgasms consumed them, until every last drop had been milked from their shaking bodies.

Panting, he collapsed on top of her as she attempted to catch her breath. Realizing he was still very much asleep, she used her might to roll him off of her. His dick slowly slid out as he fell onto his back. Lying awake, with, once again, two snoring roommates on either side of her, she smiled. Knowing neither of them would remember set her soul at ease and she no longer cared her space was limited. It was the most fun she'd had in a long time. In fact, she already planned on making sure it happened more often. Basking in the glory of the aftermath, her heart rate began to steady.

"Now that's what I call a Christmas story," she drifted off to sleep.

THE END

CHAPTER FOUR

SEDUCING PROFESSOR WATSON

Does anyone know what happens to the vaginal environment once sperm is introduced?" Taylor asked his evening class, using a pen to point to the opening of the female's reproductive system on a diagram hanging on the whiteboard. He observed many wide-eyes and jaded facial expressions, as per usual. "Anyone?"

A hand rose from behind the head of one of my older students. Knowing exactly who those delicate fingers belonged to, his chest tightened.

'Thea. Keep it cool, Taylor.'

Trying to see her face through the disheveled mane blocking his view, he leaned to the side. Having been in a college setting for almost a decade, his night classes always painted the room with a dramatic variety of cohorts. However, this particular female student's age left him guessing. Being early in the semester, he'd only been with this class for a few weeks and the effect this girl had on him left most of his nights restless.

"Yes," he choked on his suddenly dried throat and pointed to the singular hand hovering above the man's mop. Tilting his body awkwardly in the hopes of making it clear to the dude in front of her that he was trying to see someone behind him, he lost his breath when it worked and her face was revealed.

Thea was slender, yet shapely, and drop-dead, arrow to your heart, irresistible. Taylor continued to struggle to compose himself each time she walked into class. After being immediately drawn in by her piercing emerald eyes and pale silk skin, he looked forward to this class despite knowing he couldn't do anything about his inappropriate thoughts. He blinked away the trance he had found himself in in order to peel his gaze away from the power of her.

"The pH of the vagina changes in order to create a more alkaline environment. Since sperm hovers anywhere between 7.1 and 8, compared to the typical vaginal cavity keeping much lower at 3.8 and 4.5." Her voice was melodic with a hint of a French accent and her facial expressions were agonizingly mysterious.

'Fuck. She could easily be twenty, or thirty!'

"Exactly," he managed to get out.

'She knows her anatomy well. I wonder what else she has in that gorgeous head of hers. Damn it. Stop.'

She grinned, her lips full and red, and jotted something into her notebook.

Thea had on a string-strapped dress that allowed glimpses of her skin to show through the brilliant cloak of mahogany hair that surrounded her. Every strand swayed with each movement she made and he found himself longing to run his fingers through it. Which had never happened to him before in a teacher/student setting. However, this brunette beauty got to him. It took every moral fiber in his body to ignore the devil on his shoulder. It's hungry whispers screaming... 'Wouldn't you like to know what her skin feels like pressed against yours?'

'Of course, I would! But I can't!'

"Each of you will need to grab a partner and then go over to the prop table. From there, you'll take one female reproductive organ model per team and bring it back to an open lab station."

The class got to work while he took out an instructional video to project on the screen. When he turned around, he noticed the girl he couldn't take his mind off was waiting for the crowd to dissipate, standing behind the fuss before reaching for the last sculpture. She didn't appear to have a partner, which immediately gave him a wicked idea.

'I'll be her partner. That'll be fun. Nope that would be bad. Very bad.'

After all the pairs had found their places at the lab tables, he watched from the corner of his eye while hitting play on the DVD player. The girl ran her fingers over the replica as if she had a special connection with it. He straightened his posture and walked along the far side of the classroom, cutting between two tables once he reached the row she was sitting alone in.

'What are you doing, man? Stop!'

But he couldn't. He continued toward her while the class worked diligently, looking for the parts listed on their worksheets and writing down their locations. Thea filled her's out without needing to look up at the model.

'That's interesting. I've never had a student who did not need a reference to fill out this particular assignment.'

"I noticed you don't have a partner," he leaned down and placed his hand on the table beside her worksheet.

"Seems so," Thea looked up at him, no expression on her face.

"I'd be happy to assist, should you need me."

'Dude, don't talk like that!'

She paused her writing, which was without error as far as he could tell, and tilted her head to look up at him. "I think I can manage."

'Welp, that ends that! She's not interested.'

Which he was happy to learn. It would make it easier for him to stay out of trouble. A relief he never thought he'd need as he's always been professional in his career as a professor.

"Well, alrighty then, young lady," he tapped the table twice with his palm, "let me know if you change your mind."

He walked back to the front of the room, with his proverbial tail between his legs, to check his phone while the class finished. He knew he had about twenty more minutes before that happened, so he pulled up Grub Hub and checked out his delivery options. He was suddenly ravenous and the forty-five minute commute home would leave him with little time to prepare anything other than a bowl of cereal, or left-over chicken cacciatore from the delivery the night before.

Feeling the ever-so-slight sting of rejection, he lifted his head to look over the room. Immediately directing his gaze to where she had been sitting. To his surprise, she was no longer there and her sculpture had been returned. He jolted upright in his chair, looking around the room like a frantic lunatic.

'Why am I so fucking manic over this broad?'

Then he saw her walking through the rows of desks, keeping her focus on him.

"Finished," Thea's voice slithered through the air as she slid her worksheet across the aged-wood desk until it was directly in front of him.

"Impressive," he managed to get out, nodding at her. Holding his stare a little longer than suitable for such an exchange. Her face was inquisitive as if she was trying to figure out his next move. He cleared his throat, "Have you taken many anatomy classes in the past?"

"You could say that," each syllable escaped her ruby red lips in a purr and he realized she possessed every quality a woman needed to completely take over a man's soul. He knew right then and there that he'd need to keep himself in check at all times or else his urges might get the better of him.

She blinked and lifted her chin slightly before turning to head back to her seat. Despite the commotion now ensuing all around the room, he couldn't take his eyes off of her hips as they swayed through the bustle. His crotch tightened and he could feel his dick move under the restraint of his pants, knowing full well that the only way to halt his desires was to look away, but taking his focus from the way her cheeks bobbed underneath that dress was not something any man would be able to do easily. He swallowed hard.

"Professor Watson?" A female voice yanked him from his thoughts and back into the room. He jolted his head toward a curvy blond dressed in shorts and a halter top.

"Yes," he blurted involuntarily, "all finished?"

"Almost," she leaned forward and rested her elbows on his desk, exposing her cleavage. She licked her lips, "I can't seem to figure out this part of the diagram."

"Where is your partner?" He asked her, diverting his eyes from her apparent ploy of temptation.

"He's useless," she rounded the desk and shimmied her body closer to his and pretended to need help. "Plus, I know you can help me."

Without thinking, he looked up and noticed Thea was putting on her jacket and packing up her belongings. He looked at his watch and realized there was still fifteen minutes left of class. Something strong inside of him didn't want her to leave. He needed to figure out a way to answer the student's question and return her back to her table before it was too late.

"Yes, I can help you, but the point of this assignment in particular is for me to see what you do, and do not, know." He began to stand, making sure his semi-bulge wasn't too visible through the thin fabric of his khakis. "Please try a little longer, and I promise after I go over each paper, I'll discuss all the mistakes during the next class."

He was dismissive, causing her to pout and reluctantly go back to her seat. Knowing the object of his attention was gearing to leave, he left his desk without haste and went out into the hall to get a drink of water from the fountain. Figuring she'd walk by him on her way out.

'What am I doing? I'm acting like a teenager!'

He couldn't help it. She was that stunning. Sure enough, there she was. Tall, slender and mysteriously hypnotic. She stopped in her tracks when he made eye contact with her, wiping the water from his chin. She seemed unfazed by his attempt to be sexy.

"Leaving early?" Asking the obvious was a specialty of his.

"Yes," Thea didn't take her eyes off of him, even when he stood upright and stepped toward her. "I'm feeling a little off and figured my work was done, so…"

"I'm sorry to hear you aren't feeling well, Thea," his hand twitched as he watched her mouth move as she spoke. It didn't help that her accent coiled his insides up in knots.

"It's fine. It's just a minor headache."

"Too bad I'm your teacher," he had a plan, "because I give a mean shoulder and neck massage that can rid even the nastiest of migraines. My mother used to suffer with them before she passed."

"Oh, I'm sorry for your loss," she placed her palm on her heart.

"Thank you," he stepped closer, but maintained a healthy distance.

"A massage actually sounds amazing," she moved her hand to the back of her neck and grabbed hold. "I've had a kink right here for almost two weeks now and can't manage to release it on my own. I've called several massage parlors but no one has any openings until next week."

He couldn't believe his ears. An unintentional offer to show his chivalrous side was the exact thing he needed. "This may sound odd but, how old are you?"

Thea looked up at him curiously, "twenty-three."

"I only ask because, I'm happy to try and work it out for you after class. But only if you're comfortable with that. I promise to keep this professional."

'Stop defending yourself, man. Let her answer!'

"That sounds wonderful," she started for the stairwell. "I'm going to put my things in my car, then I'll come back up. That way it doesn't look suspicious to the other students that I'm coming back in right after leaving."

The students' voices in the classroom started to elevate as class was moments from ending. "Sounds good. I have some cleaning to do so take your time."

"Okay, thank you so much," her demeanor had completely shifted. A once off-limits being he only planned on dreaming about, had transformed into an actual possibility. Something he knew was dangerous.

She exited the hall, and he returned to the room. Trying to keep his expression low-key, though the anticipation that was building inside of him was far too great to measure. He couldn't believe in only a few short moments he'd have his hands on her.

'What have I done?'

The students left one by one, each putting their collective work in a pile on his desk. The blonde was last, winking and giving him a 'your loss' look.

"See you next week, Professor Watson," she purred.

"See you," he was used to students acting that way. Especially in a college setting.

After about five minutes, and silence filled the school, he heard a door open and close somewhere in the building. His heart was about to explode in his chest and his hands were shaking. Shoving a piece of gum into his mouth, unsure of why, considering he only intended to massage her kinks. He watched the door, manically.

Precisely twenty seconds later, her hair blew into the frame of the door in what seemed like slow motion, followed by the rest of her. He was speechless. She walked into the room wearing an oversized sweatshirt and a skirt made of fleece.

"You changed." Pointing out the obvious was a specialty of his.

"I think part of the issue was the bra I was wearing. Fortunately, I had this in the car. I couldn't wear that trap a second longer. This knot is literally killing me."

"I'll see what I can do," he swiveled his chair so the seat was facing her. "Have a seat. Actually, would you mind closing the door? I don't want anyone getting the wrong idea should they walk by."

"Of course," she did as he asked without hesitation. Leaving them in total secrecy. Once she was seated, he was left standing behind her, suddenly nervous. "Should I put my hair up?"

"Yes," he choked on his words, "sorry, yes. If you don't mind."

He watched as she grabbed it with both hands and twisted it into a spiral before clipping it with a massive clasp she had clinging to her top. He let his eyes trail down toward her neck and immediately began to salivate. Jesus man, get a grip! It was perfectly shaped with a trail centered in the middle that called to his finger.

'Focus.'

"Sorry if my hands are cold," he slowly brought them to her shoulders and placed both his thumbs at the junction of each. "I'm going to feel around for tightness, but please let me know if you want me to stop at any point. I want you to be comfortable."

"I'm fine. Go as deep as you need to," she whispered and he nearly lost his balance.

'Don't whisper those words...ever, again.'

He closed his eyes and tried to keep himself in check. The moment his skin came into contact with hers, he felt he'd crossed the line. The countless videos and seminars on what's appropriate conduct between a teacher and student were apparently a waste of time. He wasn't sure why she had such an effect on him, and he wished she didn't, but this was too exciting to turn away from. Her body was warm, heated, and the way her neck melted beneath his touch made him want to continue even further. Digging his thumbs into her body and massaging the tension from her muscles was as far as he knew he'd get with her. However, her moans made it hard for his arousal to stay at bay and his thoughts to remain in control. He needed a minor distraction before his mind was completely sucked up into this sudden animalistic need growing inside of him.

'Dude, take it easy.'

"That feels so good," she breathed, letting her head drop forward and taking in all he was giving. "You have no idea how badly I've needed this."

"Happy to help," he adjusted his stance to make room for his growing dick.

'Please stay down!'

But he knew it was way too late for that. His imagination had completely taken over, painting an entire scenario in his head that he couldn't turn off.

"Fuck!" She blurted, making his eyes pop out. "Right there. Mmmmm."

He knew right then and there he'd do anything she'd ask. Every single sound that escaped her mouth sucked him further and further under her unorthodox command. He was past the point of no return and could feel his resolve fading. Moving his hands outward to caress both of her shoulders in a tight squeeze, she lifted her head and let it fall back. Almost hitting his erection. He popped his ass out of the way, but immediately became engrossed in her facial expressions, that were now right below him. Her eyes were closed and her lips parted. He could see the pinkness of her tongue and had to swallow down the dampness that filled his mouth. Imagining sinking his growing dick down her throat, he was now rock hard and needed to find a way to pull himself from the situation before he ended up fired.

"Okay," he patted her gently on both sides and quickly turned to rush to his desk so she wouldn't see what she did to him.

"Really? Already?" She faced him, confused. "That was fast."

"Sorry, I," he fumbled his words, "shouldn't be touching you, let alone causing you any sort of physical relief like that."

She stood. Slowly. Not taking her eyes off him.

'What's happening? Oh God I know that look. Don't do it...'

"What are you doing?" He spoke nervously, the head of his penis swollen and dripping. Taking the stack of papers in his hands, he tried to conceal his erection with it.

"I want more," her eyes were filled with intent, and he felt it. She continued to approach him.

"I really don't think it's a good idea to continue," he tried to speak clearly but his urges made his words sound jumbled.

"I'll be the one to decide whether or not it's good," she pushed the chair toward him and looked down between his legs. "Please have a seat. It's only fair I return the favor."

'Oh God yes. NO!'

"Thea," he tried to sway her, "really. I'm fine and don't need any sort of reciprocation."

"Please sit, professor," her seductive tone penetrated his flesh and trapped him in a state of obedience.

Sitting, he closed his eyes. Knowing he shouldn't. Biting her lower lip, she dropped to her knees.

"You don't have to do this," he could barely breathe.

"No, you see," she undid the button of his pants and pulled down the zipper, revealing the hardness she was after. "I do have to."

"Thea," his eyes closed as her hand reached into his pants and gripped the base of balls.

"Professor," she continued to explore every bulge and thickness he was carrying between his legs. Seemingly eager to learn all that she could about him.

Just when he thought she was going to take his dick out and suck the hell out of him, she stood. While he sat, panting, she let her tongue slide out of her mouth and trail across her lips, staring at his trapped erection. Taking her right hand, she touched her knee softly and trailed it up her leg and under her skirt. Taylor sat in a complete trance, involuntarily shaking his head side to side in an attempt to feign a moral compass. However, his erection continued to pulse, begging to be touched.

"What are you doing?" He whispered, not wanting her to stop, but also fearful of losing everything.

"I believe you know exactly what I'm doing," she reached the junction between her legs and rolled her head to the side as she began playing with herself.

"Please," he breathed, "don't...do that."

"Alright," she lifted her head and let her hand fall.

Thankful for her cooperation, he started to feel minor relief. However, that lasted only a few fleeting seconds before she started toward him. With Taylor remaining seated, she tilted her head to the side and spread her legs apart. His hands curled into a fist, clutching onto his pants.

"Touch me," she spoke with need.

"I can't," his body began to tremble. The pain radiating in his crotch grew the thicker he got.

"Allow me," she was not having any of what he was saying. She lifted one of her legs and stepped over his, followed by the other leg. Standing over his lap, she teasingly lifted her skirt. Exposing her dampened silk panties.

"Jesus," he blinked rapidly, finding it difficult to control his breathing.

Thea lowered her body until the crest of his bent erection subtly grazed the tip of her soft lips. Each of them fully clothed, she kept her eyes locked on his as she began to move her hips back and forth. Rubbing herself gently over him. His fingers threatened to release his pants and grab on to her, but he fought hard to keep in control. She tilted her hips forward so her clit was now getting the attention it craved against the trembling of his cock.

"Oh fuck," he moaned and grabbed hold of her ass with both hands. Feeling her move and allowing her to have her way with him while he remained still. He wanted to grind up into her more than he's ever wanted anything, but enjoyed her rhythm while he could. The fabric between her legs seeped with her excitement and through his boxers, the warmth of it sending him to the point of no return. Gripping her harder, he slammed himself up against her as he joined in on the gyrating. The pain was real but the pleasure was undeniably too good to stop. Grabbing the back of the chair with both of her hands and not breaking eye contact, she started grinding him harder. Captured by her incessant moves, he shoved himself up against her as hard as he could, practically lifting his ass off the seat. "Oh, my God, Thea, we can't do this."

She slowed, but didn't stop and reached one of her hands down between them. He panted, desperately watching her as she slithered her fingers into the open fly of his pants to free his begging dick. Once the fullness of him was released, she grabbed on to it and pumped him gently while massaging his balls with her wet, still covered, pussy.

"Fuck, fuck," his eyes rolled back into his head as he clenched his ass, trying not to explode all over them. "Stop. You have to...stop. Fuck."

She stopped. Leaving him gasping for air and visibly tormented. With a wicked smirk and a nibble of her lip, she resumed sliding herself up and down the length of his exposed shaft. Taylor clutched her lower back, following her lead. Falling deeper and deeper into her seduction. Convincing himself that since she wasn't naked, they weren't really breaking the 'no sex with students' rule. Her underwear was practically soaked and he could feel her plump lips slip free from the sides of the silky fabric with each forward push she made. He was hanging on by a thread and used every ounce of restraint to keep from exploding. Her panting and growling didn't make it easy and when she placed the heels of her shoes on the lower chair rungs, taking her off the floor, the added weight onto him was almost too much to bear. He wanted to get lost inside of her but knew this was as far as it should go.

Her body began to vibrate and her thrusts more incessantly as she continued to bring herself closer and closer to climax. She couldn't stop. With her eyes once again looking deep into his, she paused. Gasping for air.

"Are you okay?" He was barely audible.

Thea lifted herself and teased the opening to her against the tip of his penis. Pushing her entrance, although still protected by the thin material, against his swollen head. Swirling around it and causing his knuckles to turn white with need as they gripped her sweatshirt.

"Careful," he begged. But she didn't listen. She reached around her back, keeping herself directly in position for penetration, and grabbed hold of him. Holding his dick firm for her to tease. "Thea, we...can't do this."

She slowly moved her hand up and down while submerging as much of him as she could inside of her. He moaned and lost part of his vision when her tight walls squeezed around him through her panties. The skin of his shaft was taut and his balls couldn't hold in the accumulation of cum he'd been creating since the beginning of class. Combined with her flowing juices, the sounds of their bodies playing filled the air.

Being reckless, she rose to get him out of her and lifted a finger away from his dick to slide her lingerie to the side. He looked up at her and shook his head. "We can't."

"Just a little bit," she touched her greedy pussy to his dripping tip and sank down until the ridge of it forced its way inside of her. She cried out in ecstasy and he grabbed hold of her back and covered her mouth with his other hand.

"Shhh," he scolded while the girth of him stretched her, "there are still...people in the building."

They panted inches from each other's mouths and continued pushing the limits with their sex. She lifted herself so he could fall back out of her and then rubbed her wetness up and down the length of him, attending to her clit once again.

"Oh my God you feel so fucking good," he pumped his dick through her folds, feeling each time the edge of his head made contact with her sensitive nerve. "I could do this...all night."

She could feel her orgasm once again approaching so she repositioned herself to get his penis back inside of her. This time a little further. Still holding onto her panties, he was more helpful this time around getting back inside of her.

"Just the tip," he warned, "that's as far as we go."

She brought her head down so their cheeks touched and she whispered in his ear, "just a little deeper." And lowered a little more before coming back up to the top again.

"Jesus Christ!" His nails dug into her back as he popped in and out of her, coming close to exploding. "You're so fucking tight!"

"I want all of you inside of me," she lowered again.

"We shouldn't," he talked but neither was listening.

"Fill me," she went lower and he grabbed hold of her hips to try and keep her at bay.

"No one will know."

He began pumping into her fast, but only at a quarter mast. "How does that feel."

"Make me come," she bit his lip and their bodies collided fully.

He growled into the air and stood from the chair, taking her with him and slamming her onto the desk. Lifting one of her legs to the side, he used his other hand to tease her clit while plunging all he had inside of her. Barely able to keep his composure, she bucked from his touch. He pushed his dick in and out of her and could feel each pulse her walls made as he delivered stimulation to all the right places.

"Do you like that?" He pressed her clit and slammed himself through the snugness of her pussy.

"Yes," she gasped for air and reached under her top to grab one of her breasts.

His thumb circled her growing nerve and his balls began to contract. Faster and faster, he toyed with her until she screamed, her climax gushing all over him. Watching her face twist and turn red, combined with the excruciating pressure her walls suctioned onto him, he was finished. She continued to pump his dick with her flesh as her orgasm shattered her, causing him to erupt with more force than he's ever experienced before. Holding himself deep inside of her as every last drop left his body, trickles of sweat falling from his forehead and onto her stomach.

Before releasing the hold he had on her leg, they watched each other's breathing. Slowly lowering her leg, he carefully pulled himself out of her and helped her up. Standing with his, still, rock hard cock, she smiled and fixed her clothes.

"I can't believe that just happened," he panted, trying to get himself back into his pants.

"You can't?" She joked.

"I mean," he twisted her skirt back into the right direction, "I'm not complaining."

"I would hope not," she mused.

"This, was okay, right?" He wanted her to reassure him and tell him that it was all good.

"It was more than okay," she smiled and grabbed her bag off the floor. "Unfortunately, I won't be making it to class anymore."

His face went beet red, "excuse me?"

"You understand." She stood upright, confident and sure of herself, "I had to do this. I work nights and can't come to class. So, now that I've secured an A, it will no longer be an issue."

His eyes bulged out of his head as she turned to walk away.

"Wait," he was practically speechless, "this was all...for an A?"

"Yes," she winked, red cheeks and all, "well, it was also for fun. But mostly for the A."

And she left...leaving him flabbergasted and spent. Knowing he'd never see her again, and that he absolutely had no other choice than to give her an A, he wasn't sure how to feel. Shocked was the front runner. He nodded to nobody and grabbed his things before flicking off the light and closing the door behind him. When he turned around, the other female student was sitting against the wall right outside the room.

If she hadn't spoken, he may have died right then and there of a heart attack, "My turn."

THE END

CHAPTER FIVE

GYM SHADY

Joel walked down the dimly lit hallway toward the front doors of the gym, running his fingers through his hair. There was a melancholy about him, and he just couldn't shake it. He couldn't get his new client, Katherine, out of his thoughts no matter how hard he tried, and he didn't know why. Sure, she was hot, but he'd seen many attractive women in his day, yet none had ever left such a permanent place of obsession in his mind as much as she did. It went deep, primal. Even something as simple as making eye contact with her sent ripples of need rushing throughout his body, and lately, his daily tasks were taking a back seat to his need to be near her. Her laugh. Her smile. The way she looked at him each time they crossed paths. Even now, long after she'd left for the day, the effects she left behind lingered inside of him. He knew he needed to get her 'out of his system'. Especially after those red silk leggings she wore today. All he could see in his mind was her, and from there his imagination went wild. He inserted the key into the glass doors to lock up for the night before his workout. Being in back all day, he hadn't realized it had started raining so hard. Flashes of lightning lit up the parking lot and that was when he noticed her car.

"What the hell? Why is your car still here?" Confused, he immediately went for his phone and sent her a message. They had been flirting over text for a while, which was part of the reason she had become so engrained in his system. Are you still here? His fingers were clumsy with nervous excitement. He waited impatiently for her to receive it, watching diligently for 'delivered' to change to 'read', but after a few minutes of nothing, he decided to skip his workout and search for her instead. Just in case.

The silence of the gym filled the air and only intensified the buzzing in his head. Walking back down the hall, he passed the men's locker room and made his way toward the weight area. Before he got there, he heard a peculiar sound coming from the women's locker room, which was odd considering the place was supposedly empty. This confirmed his suspicion that she had, indeed, stayed. Who else could it be in there? Knowing full well the cleaning crew didn't come until the early hours of the morning, so that wasn't the source. Then, he heard what sounded like a shower door opening and closing. He decided to poke his head into the opening of the ladies' room to get a better listen, holding his breath. The shower! No fucking way is she taking a shower. Naked. Wet. Damn!

Maybe it was someone else? His chest began to heave, and his throat restricted. He knew, the way he was feeling at the moment, there was only one thing that was going to come out of this. Is this really it? Is this really going to happen? She chose to stay. Why tonight? Of all the nights? He had so many questions, but the anticipation of what he hoped was about to happen over powered his need for answers. They would be alone. For the first time since meeting. Something he had hinted at wanting but lacked the guts to make a move. Their relationship had been a mostly jovial friendship, so the reality was, he wasn't quite sure how she saw him. He wanted to go in more than anything, but if it wasn't her he could get his ass fired, or even arrested, for creeping up on an unsuspecting member while they were in the bathroom. Naked. However, deep down he knew. He could feel it. Which, of course, was the hair that broke the camel's back. He was now rock hard, visualizing the woman he craved rubbing herself up and down with soapy water.

His heart rate couldn't take the suspense any longer. Fuck it. He made his way inside and inched along the row of lockers leading to the shower room. He froze in place when he noticed a trail of clothing leading toward the wash area, mostly due to the fact that one of the items was a pair of red silk leggings. Which he knew without a doubt, were hers. When he looked up, he noticed the glass to one of the doors was coated with steam, and behind it was the silhouette of a female body. Her body. She moved seductively, as if she knew he was in there. He envisioned in his mind the skin of her backside turning a torturous shade of pink from the scalding water. I sure hope she wants me as badly as I want her. He crept forward, like a predator stalking its prey, until he was only a few inches from the glass that separated him from her dripping wet body.

Panic began to sink in. What am I doing? He lowered his hand before reaching the handle of the door. This is madness! Just because she's here doesn't mean she wants to be walked in on while showering. Which, if he were to open it, their bodies would finally meet skin to skin, guaranteed. But what if he was wrong? What if she just needed a shower and had no intention of having after-hours fun with him? He turned to leave, but bent down to pick up her thong, squeezing it in his hand, he rose it to his face and inhaled her in. Closing his eyes in order to process how horny her scent made him, he knew he needed to get out of there. With a heavy sigh, he shook his head fiercely and dropped the panties to the floor before bolting out of there.

This, this is the problem. What gives me the right to waltz in there and take what I want without even an invitation? What sort of asshole am I actually?

He was deeply conflicted. He wanted nothing more than to turn his month-long fantasy into a fruitful reality, as it had in his dreams many times. His body slumped against the hall wall, letting the agony of time crawl by.

Fuck. He tried to blink away the image of her wet naked body from his mind. Of course, with the throbbing in his pants, he couldn't. All he could see were droplets of water cascading down her spine and flowing in between the crests of her ass. Her rosy, beautifully soft, ass. His knees weakened at the thought of her palms resting flat against the shower wall and her taut nipples coated in silky gel as it dripped down her stomach. He swallowed the lump in his throat and reached down to adjust the pain of arousal between his legs. Stay professional man. It's not her. She left a long time ago. Regardless of his reasoning, he couldn't avoid caressing his dick even though he knew he was out in the open and could easily be seen should someone walk by outside. He pulsed in all the right places and knew that if he didn't stop soon, he'd need to release the tension. For a moment, he thought he'd need to duck into the men's room to take care of business, but the shower shut off, distracting him from the idea. He could hear the glass shower door open, followed by one of the locker doors. The vibrations echoed through the deserted hallway and straight through his skin. His heart was about to explode, along with his cock, yet he couldn't for the life of him gain composure.

This has to be a dream.

He pressed his back firmly against the wall for stability because he knew she'd be coming out any second and he'd need to dig deep to remain professional. His anticipation was visible through his shaking hands. Any second, Katherine...

Oh. My. God. It's her. Heat tingled his face and neck when their eyes collided. Her wet hair, splayed across her bare shoulders, tempted him even further into a manic state of desire. She was wearing the same red leggings and a matching bra that she had on earlier and he couldn't peel his eyes away from her heaving breasts. He swallowed and tried to speak.

"What are you doing here?" His words were as shaky as his body and his dick pulsed for her answer.

"I think you know," She replied with a husky need in her voice and closed the gap between them. "For a private lesson, of course."

She practically floated toward him. He could smell cucumber and danger the closer she got. His blood boiled and his vision turned singular at the request. She was all he could see.

"What would you like a lesson in?" he asked, his upper back pressing strong against the wall as if he were about to fall off a cliff.

"Well, I'm really tight." She closed the gap and looked down at his erection. "What has you all...happy?" His fingers gripped the tile. He looked over to the front of the gym at the wall of glass windows by the entrance and knew this probably wasn't the best place to play cat and mouse. He was barely hanging on by a thread and needed to move her to the back of the gym, where no one would see them. Am I really doing this?

He grabbed her arm and led her over to the main arena. "We're safer here."

"Safer?" Her right eyebrow lifted slightly as she smirked, slowly removing her arm from his grip.

"Yes, safer. We don't typically give private lessons after hours and I don't want to get fired." His voice was urgent, and he could tell she was feeding off his obvious coyness. The expansive space was silent and only lit by a dim lamp coming from one of the offices behind them. "Where are you most...tight?"

She bit her lip and smiled. Please don't do that. She didn't answer him the way he was hoping. She was playing. God is she good.

"Here," she trailed the back of her hand up the side of her left ass cheek, never taking her eyes off him. She slightly turned her body so he could get a better glance. "Right here. See?"

"Lay on your back," he growled, unintentionally, and grew harder by the second. He clenched his teeth as she obeyed his demand, his mouth saturated. Once she was on her back, she spread her legs and slowly looked up at him. When the bulge inside his pants bobbed, she bit her lip once again and tossed her head to the side. His eyes were fierce and focused as he lowered himself toward her feet, making sure not to lower his gaze off of her face. She was a visual delight and the closer he got to touching her, the more dramatic her chest quivered. He wrapped his hand around one of her ankles and pushed her leg forward, bending it at the knee. She moaned. Don't fucking moan. Jesus God, woman. "Tell me if the pressure gets too much."

"Do I have to?" Her head was back and he could see the blood pulsing through the vein in her neck. He wanted to sink his teeth into her.

Fuck it. He lifted her foot up and slowly pushed her leg over her head using his body against her hamstring for added weight bearing. She was practically in a full forward split, leaving his face inches from hers. Their eyes met and, like magnets, neither of them could break the connection. His arousal hovered right above her center and it took all of his might to not press himself into her. But that didn't last long when she arched her hips and grazed his erection between her legs. She shivered and moaned.

"Careful," he whispered with a heavy breath. He could feel her heat through his pants and almost passed out from the blood rush leaving his upper body. It was too late, the thinness of her leggings made every bump and curve of her that much more noticeable, and tangible. Her lips hugged his cock through his sweatpants and left a trail of moisture as he continued to press his hips harder and harder into her. Making sure not to go full pressure, yet.

"Yes, right there," She panted and begged. "Feel free to go a little harder."

"Stay still." He demanded with confidence, rubbing his erect dick, now more deliberately, against her growing clitoris. She tried to pull his entire body down onto her by wrapping her other leg around him, but he was much stronger than she was, and he didn't want the tease to end just yet. He strategically placed his leg over hers to keep it restrained. "I said, stay still."

She let out a breath and locked her eyes to his. He alleviated her from some of his weight by lifting himself up just enough so he was able to swerve his hips and press the head of his cock against her heated entrance. Placing one of his arms around her up-stretched leg and the other on the floor bent alongside her cheek, he continued to push his tip into her until she began trembling beneath him. He wanted very much to rid themselves of their clothes, but watching her struggle was far too addictive. It was as if he was in a trance, hypnotized by her appeal. Watching every twitch, every lip bite, and every swallow she made with even the smallest of movements was worth the build-up in his pants. The fire emanating between her legs alone signaled every nerve in his groin to pump more and more blood into his shaft. As much as he wanted to make this moment linger, he quickly realized he was hanging on by a thread when the lips between her legs clenched against his dick. The act caused his skin to break out in a sweat. He curled his fingers tightly around her ankle in the hopes of regaining some control, but he was well past the point of no return.

She made herself twitch again.

"Careful," he closed his eyes and begged, pushing himself further into her soaked pants. Despite being separated by clothes, entering her, even this way, made every single one of his muscles break out into an electric frenzy.

"Why," she cried, "We've already gone this far."

His hand loosened and traveled down the length of her leg toward her knee, she squirmed beneath him. Fuck. Stop moving. But also, keep moving. She swerved and began rubbing against him the second she positioned her clit in the sweet spot. Feeling her body vibrate made his eyes twitch and roll back into his head. Her moans lulled him into a state of ecstasy and, without even being aware of it, he continued to rub his length up and down her, feeding her need as well as his own. Humping on the floor of the once bustling gym. The skin around his sac tightened as the friction they were making became more deliberate and incessant. He needed to slow things down. Things were starting to culminate inside of him. Her lips were wet and her cheeks red with desire, calling to him. She slowly lifted both of her arms up over her head, causing her chest to rise closer to his face.

"You're wearing too much clothing," he growled into her neck, moments from going primal and ripping off all her clothes with his teeth. But, before he had anything to say about it, she lowered her hands and placed them softly against his cheeks. The gentleness of it caught him off guard and in his distraction, she managed to free her leg from underneath his. She then wrapped it around his lower back before rolling him over and getting on top of him in a martial arts move fit for the movies. His hands fell to his sides in shock, impressed with her flawless role reversal. He wasn't expecting that. She sat upright and lifted her sports-bra over her head, freeing two perfectly shaped breasts that bounced with each move she made. His sights landed on her nipples, hard and calling for his tongue but the circular motion of her hips against his dick made it impossible for him to move. Taking from him what she wanted. "Oh my God."

He was close to exploding, but watching her move on top of him was enough to make him hold on longer. She was stunning. He made a fist with both hands. Knowing he needed to grab on to something, anything, on her. Just as he was about to reach for her waist to help guide her grinding, she slowed her rhythm and slid her body down his like a cat. Not breaking eye contact. Her fingers dug deep into his chest before she released them to gently scratch her nails over his stomach. His breathing quickened, knowing what she was about to do and the throbbing between his legs sent blood gushing through his ear drums. Oh, my fucking God. Yes...

She placed her hands on his sweatpants, directly over his dick, and began caressing it before moving them upward toward his tip, where she noticed pre-cum seeping through the thin cloth of his pants. Tracing the outline of his cock with her finger, she cupped his balls with her other hand while flicking her nipples side to side against his legs. "Take it out." He blurted. Her eyes narrowed and she lowered her head to kiss it as it begged to be free. Her mouth was warm. "Please, take it out."

"Patience," she whispered. Using her nose, the heat from her tongue, and her fingers, she explored his length, and curve, with fervor.

"Fuck!" he yelled.

She teased at the elastic band of his pants and toyed with lowering it. Using her teeth to lift up his shirt, she snaked her tongue around his bellybutton before flicking it under the fabric. Without even touching the head of his dick, his balls began to stir. He knew the second she placed those lips on him, he'd explode. Which was not what he wanted, yet. Despite the primitive need to come, he needed to slow down his readiness. He had spent months dreaming about how her mouth would feel against his and this seemed like the perfect time to find out. He sat up, pulling her with him into a straddle. He put both of his hands on her face and slowly pulled her toward him. She wrapped her arms under his and around his back and allowed herself to melt into him. He touched his lips to hers, softly at first, moving back and forth across her parted mouth. She smelled like coconuts, and he wanted to devour every inch of her. Her head tilted to the side as she sucked on his lower lip. She pulled and nibbled. He closed his eyes and allowed her passion to ease his heart rate. Their mouths were wet and expressive, finally living out what seemed like an eternity of skirted desire. He could do this all night, but feeling her on top of his lap made it hard to keep still for much longer. He grabbed the back of her head and slammed her firmly against him, kissing her hard enough that she'd never forget it. Their mouths danced erotically into one another, their hands gripping the other's back. Purring into him, she swirled her tongue around his, tasting everything and refusing to come up for air. She wrapped her arms around his neck and began moving her hips back and forth over him. The feeling pushed him over the edge. He squeezed his fingers into her ass, guiding her gyrations harder against his shaft.

"I want to feel you on my tongue," she purred into their kiss before breaking the connection. He reluctantly released his grip on her, letting his head fall back as she slithered down his legs, tracing her nails along the sides of his body with intent in her eyes. She smiled up at him before plunging her soft hand into his pants and wrapping her fingers around his swollen cock. He almost erupted the moment she began massaging his shaft, but she knew how to keep him in limbo. He lifted his head to watch.

God she's gorgeous.

She licked her lips, and a moan escaped him when her wet tongue grazed the tip of his dripping dick. With his hands behind him holding him up, she spread her lips snuggly around his shaft, savoring his flavor. She wanted to please him, that much was obvious. "You taste good."

Jesus.

Her mouth gripped him tightly as she lowered onto him, taking him into her throat. The windows rattled from the storm outside, but that didn't stop her sucking. His eyes bobbed in his head and the muscles in his neck started to tense up. He was going to blow. When his arms began to tremble, she slowed her movements. She was good, but he was done playing around. He leaned forward and grabbed her under her arms, rolling her onto her back. He was now on top of her, rubbing himself between her legs and taking one of her nipples into his mouth. She inhaled and licked her lips before flinging her legs around his waist and positioned his hardness against her throbbing clit.

"Not so fast. It's my turn," he exhaled. She whimpered when he severed their contact. "Don't you worry, baby. I won't let you down."

He reached his arms back and peeled her legs off him, despite her attempts to keep the rubbing going, before removing her leggings. Once she was naked, he stared between her shaking legs with lust and hunger, almost choking on his own tongue at the glistening site. He yanked off his T-shirt and tossed it to the side before running both of his hands down the insides of her thighs, watching her face intently. His eyes rolled back in his head when her scent slithered up to him, causing his cock to grow another inch. He leaned in and trailed his tongue gently between her slit, getting a taste of her, moving up to her nerve. She squirmed, but he held her down by her sides before slamming his mouth against her. She screamed and grabbed at his hair as he sucked and swirled her tender flesh. His growls only made her more wet, but he couldn't help it, the way she tasted drove him crazy. He inserted his tongue inside of her, arching it toward the sweet spot, and pushed his upper lip against her button.

She gasped and her lungs ceased to breathe as he flicked her hidden gem while continuing to caress her clit. "I want you, now." She begged. He wanted her too, but this was too addicting to stop just yet. He could feel her pulsing against his tongue and he wanted nothing more than to feel her come into his mouth. He retreated his tongue slowly and moved back to her swollen detonator with the intention of feeling her legs quiver around him. Placing two fingers inside of her, he continued to play with her while humming and sucking her clit. It didn't take long before she hooked her feet and lifted her ass off the ground as her body began to spasm. He pressed harder and held her tighter as her orgasm ricocheted around him. With his face saturated in her release, he matched her movements with his mouth until she calmed. Panting, her legs fell off him. "Please, get inside of me."

She didn't have to ask him twice. He stood, looking down at her heated cheeks and pussy, and lowered his pants. His cock bobbed once it was free from restriction and her eyes widened. He clenched his jaw and lowered himself over her, placing his hand over her heart before burying himself inch by inch inside of her. Her grip on him was intense, making it torturously satisfying penetrating her. He groaned in pleasure at the halfway mark, needing to flex his ass to push his way in further. Her cries echoed around them as her nails ripped across his lower back, clawing at him to take her fully. His body shook as he pulled back to spread her juices over him. Being more lubed, he continued entering her, his forehead dripping with sweat. Once fully penetrated, his balls cradling her ass, they looked into each other's eyes before bringing it home. Even motionless, they could feel every twitch, squeeze, and pull their bodies made together. Her inner walls constricted and pleaded against the taut skin of his dick. He wasn't sure if he'd be able to move without spilling into her and he wanted her to come again, so he lowered his head and kissed her, hoping it would curb the edge.

It didn't.

Her lips were swollen and soft and the way she moved them against his sent waves of fever throughout his entire body. He tried his damnedest to slow the frenzy, focusing on her rather than the sensations exploding throughout him. Her cheeks were flamed, and her eyes were like liquid fire. She squeezed his body into hers and bit his lower lip before speaking.

"What are you waiting for?" Her lips moaned into his.

"Careful," he replied sincerely, "I don't know how long I can hold on." He pulled himself half-way out of her and she clung to him. He couldn't take any more of the pleasure and plunged deep inside of her. "Shit!" With each thrust, the friction was euphoric against his highly sensitive cock. He could hear their juices mixing despite the sound of her purring in his neck. That was all it took to turn him into a ravenous beast. He moved his hand off of her pounding heart and grabbed one of her breasts, clutching her shoulder with the other. It didn't take long for her entire body to build up again as he continued to drive into her. Her walls spasmed and collapsed around his dick, making it hard for him to move. She was damn powerful.

"Fuck!" He grabbed both of her shoulders now and held onto her as his whole body quivered with release. Slamming each pulse of his orgasm into her. His skin was drenched, and his muscles cramped, but the sensations wouldn't stop. Moving his hands under her ass, he squeezed each cheek with his powerful hands, continuing to empty himself inside of her. Unable to breathe. His back trembled and their feet were twisted up together as their bodies were consumed with pleasure. After what seemed like eternity, the wave began to wane. Their soaked bodies trembling as they clung to one another. When all was still, the only thing they could hear was the pounding of their hearts and the thunder outside.

"I don't know about you," she joked, "but I think private training is significantly underrated."

"Well, to be fair," he whispered into her mouth, "You haven't seen the bill yet."

THE END

Chapter Six

HER VOICE

I can't hear you, Cylvia," Adrien announced, his French accent thick with annoyance. Bringing the entire orchestra, and vocalists, to a screeching halt. "How many times must I remind you, that being primary Soprano means your voice must be heard over all others? Start again."

Though this was only their first class, the ensemble had been at it for hours. They flipped their packet to the opening number, again, while hiding their disappointment in Cylvia. Adrien signaled their restart before waving his arms. Music filled the theatre, with Cylvia nailing her vocal requirements, and the entire choral symphony was able to make it through most of their songs, apart from one. Their final number. Being newly chosen for primary, Cylvia had been riddled with panic due to Adrien's rigorous reputation, and being put on the spot and possibly holding the others back. Having little time to fill the role of the previous lead's sudden departure, his disappointment in Cylvia was palpable, and mostly unwarranted.

"I'd like to see a handful of you tomorrow morning," Adrien proclaimed once the piece was finished. No acknowledgment of their improvement. "If you see an email tonight, I expect you here no later than eight."

They collected their instruments and made their way off the stage. Leaving Adrien alone in silence. Having been a conductor for over fifteen years, his forty-seven-year-old body was growing tired of inadequate performers. News of his abilities spread far and wide after last year's show and his name rose to greatness as a result. After his feat of transforming popular rock songs into classical masterpieces in a way that has never been heard before, the pressure that comes along with that to meet expectations has proven to be quite the thorn in his side. Mostly due to the fact that nothing, and no one, seemed to elate his high standards. Having three months to prepare for his next masterpiece, he wondered after tonight's first rehearsal if he'd made a mistake in his position assignments. However, remembering the auditions, he couldn't think of anyone apart from Cylvia to fill the role. Knowing it was still early in their rehearsals, he was disappointed she didn't project her voice as he had originally anticipated she would when he agreed to take her on.

He closed his book and exited the building. Hailing a cab outside of the theatre, he was looking forward to sitting at his usual table at V's Lounge. Tucked away in a dark corner, sipping Manhattans while letting his mind go blank had become part of his routine after the many long and tiring auditions he had to sit through until compiling a top-notch grouping.

The taxi pulled up at the door within six minutes, and although it was late and raining, he couldn't help but feel a pull of excitement. On the wall beside the door was a framed poster of the evening's entertainment and he paused before entering to see who the featured singer would be. A part of him enjoyed the bluesy sounds the female performers painted the room with, but a larger part of him longed to have someone match his level of audible talent. Nonetheless, he was eager to get in there.

"Good evening Mr. Harrowmond," A gentleman in a suit greeted him as he entered, "your table is ready."

He nodded in reply and followed. Being one of the most sought-after nightclubs on the strip, his status in the area was a benefit when ensuring he'd never be without his spot. Every table was filled and the bar was like honey to bees as swarms of drinkers overcrowded the few bartenders working it. Turning the corner, which opened to the private reserve, his table was dimly lit with his drink already waiting for him. The host instinctively held out his arm to direct Adrien to his seat.

"Enjoy your time, sir," he walked away.

Throwing his things on the long half-circle booth, he tucked himself into the center so he could have a clear shot of the stage. The singer should be coming out any moment and he was looking forward to letting his mind shut down before having to endure another long day tomorrow.

A group appeared in front of the area he was in, loud and obnoxious. Waiting to see if they'd move before show time, he watched them argue over whose turn it was to buy the next round. Rolling his eyes before taking his third sip, he reached into his back pocket to retrieve his phone to check the time. As his hand made contact with the mobile device, a woman in red caught his attention. With curves chiseled by the gods themselves, she stood with sensuality, poise, and an off-the-chart level of confidence. Cutting through the crowd, he watched as all the men within the group turned their heads as she passed them on her way to the bar. He watched as she placed both of her hands on the ledge of the mahogany serving station while speaking to the doting server in front of her. After her order was complete, she turned her head toward the stage and then back around until her gaze landed directly on Adrien.

He halted his need for the time and took another sip of his drink. Their eyes locked briefly and due to the magnetic feeling that was now coursing through his body, he couldn't help but wonder if he knew her. Before breaking eye contact with him to get her order, her facial expression shifted into one of bewilderment. As if she was trying to read something written on his face. Lifting her shot glass, she downed the clear booze before slamming it back down onto the bar. A part of him wanted to go to her, even though the reason, as well as the urge, remained a mystery. However, when he went to stand, he noticed she had vanished somewhere back into the crowd. Chalking it up to being overly stressed, he sat back and closed his eyes for a moment while waiting for the evening's entertainment to begin. He had a mission and didn't have the time, nor the proper mood, to go lady hunting. At least not for the bed.

He could see the lights shift through his eyelids so he opened them and signaled the waiter to send him another drink. The crowd hushed when the microphone illuminated and out from the far back corner of the stage walked the lady in red. Having his undivided attention, he straightened his back and waited patiently for her to begin. Even when his beverage had been placed down in front of him, he remained stoic. Curious to hear her voice.

"Sir," the young server whispered, "this drink is compliments of the lady."

His focus crumbled around him at the words and he turned to face the gentleman. "Lady?"

"Yes, sir. Ms. Fiona," he nodded toward the woman on stage as she wrapped her fingers around the staff of the microphone. "Will there be anything else?"

"No," he shook his head in utter confusion and reached for the freshly made Manhattan. Looking up, he locked eyes with the mystery woman. Fiona. Bringing the glass to his mouth, he let the cool liquid drip along his tongue while they studied each other from afar.

Turning her attention to the crowd, she closed her eyes and opened her mouth. The moment her words escaped her lips, the entire bar went silent. Still like the early hours of a winter's morning. Unable to swallow the remaining liquor in his mouth, he fell into a trance weaved by each note she sang. Her body swayed seductively to the melody of her ballad and he couldn't pull his eyes away from the way the silk of her dress moved back and forth over her breasts and hips.

Lowering his glass to the table, he managed to get down the collection of booze in his throat while trying to make sense of how this woman had enthralled almost all his faculties with merely a glance and a sound. His thoughts tempted to leave him with each syllable she hummed into the air as if he were being hypnotized and his will was no longer his. His upper lip twitched when she belted out a note he had been longing to hear almost his entire professional career. His jaw dropped at the realization that this was precisely the vocalist he'd been searching for. Finding a new sense of gusto, he downed the rest of his cocktail and waited patiently for her to finish. His heart pounded in his chest at the thought of speaking to her and convincing her to join his chorus. However, he couldn't help but examine every curve and fluid movement she made, despite needing to stay professional.

Never lacking in female companionship, his hookups consisted of one-night affairs filled with him being aggressive and controlling and then never seeing them again. Unable to feel any sort of attachment, he used them to satisfy his cravings for dominance. A part of him wanted to see this lady in red tied to his bed but knew that having her be a part of his orchestra would be far more valuable to him. The combination of her voice, and the way her long red hair complimented the gown that hugged her, held a power he realized he'd have to try to avoid if he wanted his show to run smoothly. Holding firm to never cross that line, as his career meant more to him than did his own family, a performer had never even entered his fantasies. Not even for a moment. His mind simply didn't go there. He was…turned off. When he had an itch that needed scratching, he simply found a participant willing to scratch it. No desire, no lust, and certainly never any longing.

His draw to her intrigued him and he could only assume it had to do with his outlandish disappointment with Cylvia combined with the quality booze coursing through his veins. Nevertheless, there was something about her, and he'd be damned if he didn't figure it out. Taking his last sip, of the beverage she gifted him, she belted out a note so strong, so loud and so…perfectly pitched, he stopped himself from breathing until she made her way through it. The wrinkles in his furrowed brow released and the tension he'd built up over the years waned from his shoulders. He'd never heard anything remotely close to the sound with which she had just coated the room and looking around, he was convinced she was the one. Not a single soul in the bar moved and he spotted at least three women patting the tears from under their eyes with a napkin.

When she came up for air, her head returned to its front forward position yet her eyes flicked right at him as if to say, 'That was for you'. Every single strand of hair on his body stood on end and a shiver ran down him.

"What the fuck was that?" He whispered to himself as she closed the number.

The crowd erupted in applause and stood from their seats. With everyone now standing, he couldn't see her. Getting to his feet, he moved his body from side to side to try and see through the onslaught of new fans but when he finally hit the right angle, his stomach dropped. She was gone.

"No," he breathed. He panicked and knew from past experience that after a singer's final number here they would bow and leave out the back door. A ploy to leave the customers literally addicted to return in hopes of seeing them again. The draw to thrill from the mysterious. He slammed down a twenty and bolted for the door. People mingling and getting refills made his exit nearly impossible. "Excuse me."

The couple in front of him moved to the side as classic jazz filled the air. Just as he was about to turn the corner for the door, a fleeting glimpse of red caught his eye through the bustle. He froze where he stood and scanned the room in the direction he'd seen it go. Within seconds, two bodies parted and there she stood. Standing at the bar with a drink in her hand, she was looking right at him. His chest tightened and for the first time in many years, his dick twitched. Blinking away the lunacy of that reaction, he walked toward her. He couldn't help but get pissed with himself and the anxiety he was feeling. It wasn't like him at all and he needed to remember who he was. Shaking his right hand in the hopes of freeing himself from some of the tension, he saw a different sort of red when another man approached her. Slowing his stride, he watched her smile at him and pull a lock of her hair behind her ear.

Clenching his jaw, he reached the bar and positioned himself directly behind her, and tried to listen. Hoping she'd turn to face him, he suddenly felt desperate. Which angered him.

"Excuse me," he interrupted, not giving a fuck who the other guy was.

She slowly turned and when their eyes met, he couldn't speak. She smiled in a way that made him wonder if they had met sometime before. She was comfortable as if she knew him and for a brief second worried that she could have been one of his past conquests on any number of nights he'd had a few too many to drink.

"Thank you for the drink," he nodded, stoic and sure of himself, as always. Analyzing her facial features, and most certainly looking like a creep doing it, he realized there was no way he'd met her before. She was a rare beauty he would most certainly have remembered, and seeing her now was definitely a first. Taking a silent sigh to himself in relief at the knowledge of having not burnt any bridges with her, he returned to the task at hand. And nothing, other than her compliance, would stop him.

"You looked like you could use one." Her words were barely audible to him and he was drawn into a mild trance while watching her lips move and the way her tongue flicked the roof of her mouth ever-so-delicately with every syllable she spoke.

He swallowed, "Am I that obvious?"

"Hey," the guy now behind her blurted, "care to pick up where we left off?"

She went to speak but didn't get the chance to.

"Leave," Adrien demanded. Eyes dark and threatening.

The guy made a disgusted face, "Excuse me?"

"Now." It wasn't up for debate, and the guy knew it.

He looked at her, hoping for some back-up, but she just sipped her drink and smirked. He scoffed and walked away. Seemingly not interested, or afraid, to turn it aggressive, Adrien kept his focus on the back of the man's head as he disappeared down the bar. From the corner of his eye, he noticed her mouth parting with approval. Which in turn promoted his own secret smirk. Bringing his sole purpose of finding a replacement for Cylvia back to the forefront, he knew he couldn't blow his chances of hooking her. Having been trying to cast the most balanced orchestra New York has ever seen, nothing would stop him from obtaining her. She would be his primary vocalist. After almost a year and a half of searching, his chest tingled with knowing that he was mere moments from obtaining the final piece of his excruciatingly high-standard puzzle.

"Where were we?" She spoke first, searching his face and shifting her weight to the side.

The motion humored him, but only for a moment. He had foolishly led himself to believe that he had regained his authority by holding firm to his purpose, but when he noticed her nipples harden beneath the thinness of her silk dress his throat stiffened and he nearly suffocated.

Now is not the time for such fancies, Adrien. Focus. You can have sex with anyone you want, just not her. She shouldn't even be getting to you like this. He tried to redirect his primitive captivation with her to a more 'who does this woman think she is, taunting me with her curves and veering me off path with her voice?' Clenching his jaw, he flexed his facial muscles before addressing her.

"I'm glad you asked," Adrien pointed a finger up to alert the bartender he needed a refill. "A gin and tonic, please," and he turned to her, "and for you?"

"I'll have Absinthe if you have any stored in that secret cabinet of yours," she knew how to talk to people. Making them feel excited and having them believe they stood a chance. The bartender nodded with a grin and got to work. She turned her attention back to Adrien, "It's one of the only bars in the city to have it. Until someone reports them."

"My lips are sealed," his voice was deep and seductive but he couldn't quite tell if she was as equally drawn to him as he was to her. But it mattered little to him, as he wasn't interested in her for that. The drinks were delivered promptly and he grabbed both and handed her hers. "I've never seen you perform here."

"This is my second show," she placed her lips on the edge of her glass and let the green liquid coat them before she let her tongue lick away the remnants.

"Ah," Adrien took a sip of his drink, "where were you before this?"

"I'd been singing at the San Francisco Opera House for a little over ten years before deciding to come here," she shifted her body so she was square with his. As if to get a better read on him, but also allowing more of her outline to be visible. Which he noticed, painstakingly.

Focus. She's just a female. Pussy is pussy, man, get it together. Ah, but something was telling him that this particular female's pussy wouldn't be like the rest. Fuck.

The more he tried to play off his attraction and curiosity, the stronger the struggle inside of him grew. Her breasts were supple and hung freely under her fitted silk gown. Trying to keep his gaze from falling to her tastefully exposed side-boobs and imagining what it would feel like to run the back of his hand along them, he tried to keep his attention elsewhere.

"Why the drastic coast change?" He leaned toward her so she could absorb his magnificent-ness but her demeanor remained unfazed. Or so she let on, was his thinking.

"Let's just say," her face turned coy and even more mysterious than it had just been a moment ago, "I wasn't appreciated to the level I felt I had earned."

"Is that so?" He was now fully intrigued.

"It is in fact so," she giggled and took another flirtatious sip before continuing. "Let's just say I have certain standards that weren't being met."

"Why, Ms. Fiona," he flashed her a smile, "that is wonderful news."

"And how do you know my name, Mr.?" She was amused by his comment and now giving him her full attention, which he had anticipated would only be a matter of time.

"I have my ways," his jaw was strong as he looked intently at her.

"I do love a secret admirer," she winked and took a sip, "so why is it that me having high standards is good news?"

"Well, it just so happens I've been hunting for such a standard myself," he took a sip. "It hasn't been easy."

"Go on," she coaxed him. Pressing her red glossed lips together while swallowing down another sip, the effects of the emerald liquor taking root within her.

Unsure of how many drinks she had consumed throughout the evening, he was pleasantly amused with her sudden interest in what he was saying. Not to mention the way her rosy cheeks made his dick thicken. Being almost four drinks in, Adrien could tell he was rapidly losing his ability to make judgment calls. He could feel the awakening of his primitive urges and knew if he didn't make this work, and soon, he'd end up fucking her. And if that happened, he wouldn't be able to work with her. That was, and will always be, his single most observed manner of conducting business. But he was having a very hard time convincing himself that he still had his wits about him when after each time she drank her drink she'd lick her lips to savor the flavor longer. Or to tease him mercilessly, to which he was fully there for apparently and quickly needing to take it to the next level.

I need to get the fuck out of here.

"I'd love nothing more," he put his empty glass on the bar and took out a few twenties to pay their tab, and then some, "but I'm afraid I do have to get going. Can I have your contact info and I'll get in touch with you tomorrow?"

"Sounds perfect," she followed his lead and returned her empty glass, "I need a ride anyway. We can talk more on the way."

"Oh," he wasn't expecting her to invite herself into his car, since he hadn't let on that he was offering. However, he realized he should have guessed she'd do that given her impeccable show of confidence. "Do you typically get in cars with strangers?"

"You're not a stranger," she said pointedly and looked him dead in the eyes.

"You don't even know my name," he was suddenly feeling as though he had misjudged her. Any female willing to go off with a man they just met wasn't exactly the epitome of decision making he'd expect from the person he was searching for. He needed sharp, loyal, hardworking and most of all, a serious craving for perfection. So, this threw him off. However, he looked on the bright side. Now he could fuck her.

"I do, in fact, know your name," she straightened her stance, "Mr. Harrowmond."

"How do you know me?" He was pleased that his initial assessment of her was still intact with the discovery that she was aware of him. Which he should have known, given his status in this area of New York.

"I have my ways," she winked and headed for the door. Adrien followed.

Well, that settles that. Fucking is off the table. Maybe she'll give me a solo on the ride. His dick jumped. Down boy. Not this time. Not with this one. She was far too important.

"Touché," he nodded and held the door open for her to exit the bar. When they were on the road, Adrien's driver pulled up within seconds and got out to open the back door for them. "After you."

"Fancy," she purred and climbed in.

"Thank you, Stewart," Adrien ducked in after her. "Where to, young lady?"

"West 28th," her voice was angelic even in regular speech.

He hadn't been able to fully hear just how silk-like it was with the chaos of the bar. But now, in the silence of his Lincoln, he could make out every breathy articulation, the fluidity of her fluency and how every word seemed to slither out of her mouth and cast a spell around his eardrums. He was thoroughly captivated and suddenly worried he'd be unable to keep to his promise of 'hands off'.

"Well look at you," he was impressed she lived in a nice area and wondered if she'd be interested in seeing his place on Fifth Ave. But that ship had sailed once again now that she wasn't the promiscuous young lady he had worried about moments ago. "West 28th, Stew."

The car took off through the heavy late night weekend traffic. The ride would take close to an hour in this gridlock and Adrien figured he'd use the time to get her on board. Looking over at her, he watched as she looked out the window and slowly crossed her legs. It was as if she knew his eyes were on her. With her right hand, she rubbed the side of her thigh with a seductively slow stroke and Adrien's cock couldn't help but fantasize.

Shit.

Rubbing both of his hands up and down the tops of his legs, he forced the images of her kneeling between them in the darkness of the back seat out of his head.

"To get right into it," Adrien turned his body slightly to angle himself better for a conversation, "I'd be very interested in offering you the Primary on my team."

"Wow," she was visibly taken aback. "You know that after seeing only one of my shows?"

Touché

"I knew that after hearing only one of your notes," he kept his voice low and commanding as to make it known to her his seriousness.

"Smooth," she played coy and recrossed her legs. "Go on."

"I've grown tired of mediocre jezebels who promise their souls to me yet their deliverables are less than optimal," he leaned forward and grabbed two bottles of water from the side-bar. Handing her one of them, he continued, "It took less time for me to see in you what I've been looking for than it did for me to realize that I was the best goddamn conductor the world has ever seen. Which, trust me, didn't take long."

"Well, confidence is key," she winked at his cockiness and took a drink of water, "so they say."

"They aren't wrong," he was focused on reeling her in but was also beginning to feel the effects of the alcohol he had consumed earlier mixed with the 'longest ever' bout of sex deprivation he's had in a while. He needed to figure out if she was in, or not. Because if she wasn't, his next move would be ripping that red number off her curvy, begging-to-be-touched body. "It would be less than ideal to be in my line of work should I feel otherwise. Also, ticket sales give a pretty accurate read when confirming this particular high level state of mind."

"I find it to be very appealing for a man to know exactly what he wants. Without letting distractions muddle the vision," she knew exactly what she was doing. She was no dummy and was toying with his resolve.

He hadn't thought he was being obvious with his need to fuck her and how he was currently in limbo with crossing that line and potentially ruining his golden ticket to success. Which he knew was her. Listening to her sing had quite literally sent him into the exact trance he hoped his audience would fall in to and he really didn't want his dick to fuck it all up. Even if his imagination was running rampant and he couldn't get the thought of sliding his cock between her juicy, wet lips.

Stop it. Get her to join you and leave it be. I can always just use some other broad to curb the itch in the meantime.

"I'm very happy to hear that," he finished his water in the hopes of quenching his nagging thirst. "Would you like to discuss the arrangement and my proposal for compensation?"

She put the remainder of her water in the side cup holder and looked him dead in the eye. His facial features softened as her demeanor shifted right before him. He watched intently as her left hand rose to her dress strap. Sneaking one of her perfectly manicured fingers underneath the tempting material of her gown, Adrien was sent into a brief state of paralysis.

Wanting nothing more than to see her naked body and to show her all the ways he intended on using it, the proper showing of conduct was currently on hold. He was now more confused than mission driven. Typically, when it came to female activity and their response to him, he was the one baiting and directing the outcome he desired. Yet, she shifted within such a short period of time, and with no forward encouragement, that he had absolutely no idea how to proceed. Considering she was the one he wanted.

"I'd love to discuss the arrangement you have in store for me," she dragged the red silk down her arm and then switched to the other side. Keeping her eyes firmly on his chiseled and hair-shadowed face.

"What are you doing?" He had to ask. Even though he was well aware she was trying to seduce him, out of nowhere, he had to try and redirect her advances seeing as though she would be entering a professional relationship with him. And he was less than thrilled with having to ward off such an enigma of a woman. Especially with the constant onslaught of images of her straddling him, naked, with his hands squeezing her hips so hard that his fingers could barely be seen. It was bad enough trying to keep his erection from being noticed, let alone the ultimate tease he was now faced with. Not to mention the booze wreaking havoc with its rather annoying and predictable indecisive decision making. It was either constructing the most magnificent orchestra of all time or allowing his cock to be treated to the nectar of this beauty sitting before him.

"I'm making myself more comfortable," she brought her arm behind her back to bring down the zipper, but couldn't reach the toggle, "and to answer you, I'd be interested in discussing the contract."

"Listen," he struggled to breathe through the quickened progression of his arousal. *Why do I want to fuck the hell out of this woman? What about her is so captivating that I can't fucking think straight?* He didn't know the answer to either of those questions, and he wanted to be pissed off about it, but currently all his energy was being redirected to feeling what it would be like to have her on top of him. *Fuck.* "If we are going to work together, we can't..."

"I assure you I mean no misconduct, Conductor, but if I don't at least loosen this thing, I may pass out," she stopped trying to undo her dress and turned her back to him. "So do your new student a favor, and help her to breathe a little easier, would you?"

He inhaled, realizing he misread her actions, and watched as she collected her flowing mahogany locks into her hand and moved it out of the way, exposing her bare back and shoulders to him. He wanted to lean forward and sink his teeth into the side of her neck and feel her squirm, but she was now off limits. Luckily, being in this industry as long as he has, he knew all too well the trouble that can arise when mixing pleasure with business. His relief was palpable to him. Had she been coming on to him, he wasn't sure he had it in him to deny himself the courtesy of showing her what he was truly capable of. His dick however, was less easy to thwart.

Gripping the zipper in between his thumb and pointer finger, he slowly brought it down. Jasmine and mint floated from her skin and directly into his resolve, melting away at it with each clasp he released. The scent was exotic and reminded him of his stay in Morocco where he had spent most of his time surrounded by beautiful women and wine. Fuck, those were the days.

"How's that?" He had managed to get it half way down but stopped when the arch of her lower back became visible and letting his hand have its own adventure was instantly a real threat.

"A little lower should do the trick," her rib cage expanded but he could see that she was still quite restrained.

As he lowered it further, his knuckles couldn't help but graze the small of her back. A faint moan escaped her mouth and his entire body rattled with incurable curiosity. He wanted more of that sound. He wanted her skin bare so he could watch it change color before his very eyes from the workings of his palm against her soft, innocent flesh. Of course he was assuming she was innocent, having only met her this evening. But it was his fantasy and there is where he will keep her. Drawing his hand back and breaking the contact, he tried to compose himself before carrying on with the logistics of joining his orchestra.

"Better?" He practically growled the words. Clearing his throat, he waited for her to answer. Keeping her back to him, she turned her head back.

"Much," shifting back to her previous angle, they were now facing each other. With her clothing now considerably more loose, he tried to keep his sights off the very real possibility that one of her breasts could make an appearance at any moment. Swallowing, Adrien reached into his black leather briefcase and pulled out a contract. "Right back to it I see."

"It's best to lock down talent before it runs away," he handed it to her and when her arm rose to grab it, her right nipple found an escape route out of the side of her fallen shoulder strap. The feminine heft of her chest was distracting, resulting in a tingle Adrien's crotch couldn't fight. Now he was at the point of no return. He slowly brought his dark eyes up to her face and clenched his jaw when their eyes locked.

"Everything...alright?" She breathed, knowing exactly what that look entailed. Taking the papers out of his tight hold, the action resulted in her dress falling even lower. Exposing almost all of her.

"No," he whispered, "everything is not alright."

She swallowed hard and looked down at herself. Her breathing increased, which made the crests of her breasts heave and call to him. Bringing her eyes back up to him, he reached for the call button behind him.

"Unless the divider is down, don't stop driving," Adrien then flicked the switch next to it that raised the privacy slide that separated them from being seen.

When it was completely sealed, Adrian leaned forward and took the stapled forms from her hand and tossed them to the floor. Her lips were moist and parted and he knew exactly what he wanted to see them wrapped around. No longer able to control the animal she taunted inside of him, he continued to advance toward her. Crawling slowly across the back seat and up her body as she opened her legs to allow him through. As they moved backward, her once partly covered chest popped free of their confines, showing him exactly what he so desperately wanted to see. When both of his arms were supporting his weight on either side of her, she lifted her hips to press herself against his most eager part. She made a wicked face of pleasure and dared him to continue without saying a word.

She kept their eyes locked, waiting for his next move and seemingly not worried about the consequences. His cock thickened being so close to her, his body wedged between her dress covered legs, and the calling of her breasts made his visions turn primal. Leaning down, he attacked her left nipple with his mouth. Sucking it into his mouth and swirling his tongue around it until he felt it harden between his lips. She moaned out in pleasure and grabbed his silver-sprinkled hair. The stubble on his face scratched her soft skin, making it turn pink under his assault. He was going to town, digging his face into it as far as he could and grabbing the other with his right hand. She arched her back and let her right leg fall to the side, allowing his erection to fall between her legs.

"Doesn't this," she breathed, "go against the business side of things?"

He rose his head and brought his face an inch away from hers, "Yes."

She looked down at his wet, swollen lips and closed her eyes when the heat of his breath coated hers. He grabbed her upper neck with his hand and brought his other to her knee. Watching her react to his touch, he trailed his fingers up her inner thigh and underneath the fabric of her silk gown until he reached her panties. She exhaled and waited for his touch. Taking the front of her thong into his hand, he yanked it down and moved his body accordingly until it was down to her knees. Opening her eyes, she invited him in with a devilish smirk. Bringing his fingers to her small patch of pubic hair, he let his thumb sneak its way down and through her smooth lips until reaching her entrance.

"You're wet for me," he growled in her ear, biting her lobe and plunging his finger into her warmth.

She hummed and let his hand do what it wanted with her. Squeezing his hand around her neck a little harder, he used the palm of his other hand to massage her clit while his thumb stirred within her moisture. Taking her leg, she wrapped it around his legs. Allowing the flowing silk of her dress to fall and her hip to show, distracting him from his choke hold. Getting to his knees, he took all the material he was tangled in and flung it up and over her upper body, giving him a front and center view of her lower body while keeping the rest of her buried under a sea of red satin. Crouching like a tiger, and crawling underneath the bridge her panties made between her knees, he grabbed hold of her voluptuous hips with both hands. Squeezing them like dough, he bit the inside of her leg before taking his nose to her center. Inhaling the sweetness he drew out of her, his cock begged to be free and have a turn. Using his grip on her to lift her ass off the seat, he slammed his mouth around her clit and started grinding the thickness of his tongue against it.

"Oh fuck," she screamed.

It didn't take her long to start trembling but he had a plan, and letting her come now was not part of it. Releasing his suction on her, he flicked the tip of his tongue over her growing nerve with just enough pressure to keep her in place. Knowing at any moment he could make her explode, he ventured lower and sampled her flowing arousal. Hooking his tongue into her, avoiding any contact with her clit, she tried to position herself to get him on it again.

"Please," she begged, "touch me again."

He didn't answer. No one could tell him what to do and soon she would come to realize that. Trailing his lips up and down her pussy while licking inside of her, he reached down to his pants and undid his button and zipper to relieve the excruciating pain of his thickness being restrained. Once he was able to pull his dick out, still covered with his boxers, he continued with his meal while rubbing himself against the cool leather of the seat. She squeezed her legs around him in the hopes of making her clit come into contact with anything she could manage, Adrien removed his tongue from her and rose. Taking her dress and bringing it back down, she looked at him shocked and panting.

With her on her back looking up at him, he kneeled and lowered his pants to his knees. Keeping his boxers on, her eyes widened when she saw his hiding bulge. Licking her lips, she lifted herself until she was face level with his dick. Lifting his arms, he grabbed onto the treads on the ceiling of the car and watched as she moved her hands toward him. Using her fingers, she coyly played with the slit in his underwear until a part of his head came into view. Dripping and pulsing with need, she coiled her fingers around his still covered shaft and lapped up his pre-cum with her soft tongue.

"Take me inside those lips of yours," he demanded, still hanging from the bar above and on his knees.

But she wanted to give him a piece of the same medicine he had refused to give to her, he knew it. He allowed her to continue with her tease, as that was perfectly fine with him. The car barely moved within the traffic surrounding them and while she circled her tongue around his tip, he watched the vehicles outside creep by. Running over a small pothole, the turbulence caused half of his dick to fall free and into her hand. The warmth of her palm made his neck fall back and his eyes roll in his head.

"Squeeze me," he growled. She gripped him harder and he began pumping himself through her clutch and against her pressed lips. "Open your mouth."

She let her jaw fall just enough to wedge his head into her damp mouth and the tightness she made with her lips made his entire body spasm and pump harder. Without letting him go deeper into her, she toyed with him until he started to see red. Unable to take it any longer, he broke their play and sat on the seat. Moving her legs away from him, he pulled out the entirety of his dick. Once the cloth was out of the way and nestled at the base of him, she reached forward and pulled her panties down to her ankles before slamming her on top of him in a straddle.

Her clit and pussy pressed against his shaft and held it against his body and he reached under her dress to grab her ass. Once he had a solid hold of her, he began to slide his dick up and down her while her nipples freely rubbed against his buttoned down shirt. Looking down between them, he watched as their bodies rubbed together. Her moans and wetness filled the silent space of their ride as he pushed down on her with his arm strength to add more friction to their humping. She started to tremble and he couldn't contain the build up of fluid inside of him. Leaking all over her, he slowed his grinding before she came.

Trying to back away from her, she incessantly kept trying to get off on him. She was close and so was he. Grabbing the base of his cock, he positioned it at her entrance and once it was clutched by her lips, he grabbed both of her hips and slammed her down on him. She screamed loud enough for the driver to hear and Adrien circled her body around his shaft to spread their combined moisture. The tightness of her almost ended their half-naked union too soon so he controlled their movements until he had a better grasp of himself. Just when he thought he was back in control, she tightened her walls around him and began bobbing up and down on him.

"Fuck you," he grunted and began pounding her hard. She reached up and grabbed the same bar he had held on to earlier and let him attack her body however he wanted. Flinging her around like a rag doll, he continued to hammer into her with enough power to have her head hit the ceiling. The car bounced like it was on hydraulics and when his balls began to coil, and his crotch tightened, he flung her down onto her stomach and flung her dress over her body so he could see her ass. Glistening with their fucking, he grabbed his cock and rubbed it all around her pussy and ass hole. Spreading their lube, he began to enter her puckered hole. She grunted and reached forward to stabilize herself. Taking his other hand, he submerged three of his fingers back into her pussy while circling her clit with his thumb. She cried in pleasure and he continued to bury himself into her ass. Inch by inch he entered her tight canal while supplying her with enough stimulation to get her as close as he was.

Now being full-tilt, he stilled. Swerving his hips side to side to ensure she was properly coated before bringing them both home. When she started moving slightly back and forth against his fingers, he pulled himself out and plunged back in. Repeating this a few more tantalizing times, he snared his teeth each time the ridge of his dick flicked against each smooth notch within her ass. Feeling her slickness increase on his fingers and on the taut skin of his shaft, he couldn't wait any longer. Now fucking full force, he consumed all her holes and gave her clit the attention it so desperately needed as their bodies began to vibrate. Feeling the rush of blood to his cock, he laid down on top of her and pressed himself into her as deep as he could go. Her walls collapsed around his fingers, harder than he had ever felt before, as she screamed into the seat of the car under the pressure of his body. When the inside of her ass began to pulse against his cock, he erupted without warning and roared into the air. Holding her cheeks tightly against his pelvis while he poured into her.

Grinding in unison until every spasm firing off inside of them ceased and their muscles relaxed and calmed. Sweat dripped off Adrian's forehead and onto her bare shoulders as he collapsed on top of her. Removing his fingers from her drenched pussy but keeping his dick in place, he brought his hand up and licked them clean.

"Mmmm, you taste as sweet as you sound my dear," he panted into her ear as his cock softened inside of her.

"I'm glad you approve," she answered coyly and closed her eyes.

Slowly lifting himself off her, he let his dick roll out from between her ass cheeks before giving her a somewhat firm love tap. Being a gentleman, he brought her panties back up to where they belonged as she lay in bliss. Bringing her dress back down over her legs, he helped her slowly back into a seated position before attempting to find the right words to say.

"Well," he lifted the contract off the floor and placed it on her lap, "that took a turn."

"Indeed," she exhaled and wrapped her fingers around the edges of the, now slightly mangled, pieces of paper.

"I'd still like to have you on my playbill." He knew he fucked up, but didn't regret it. Having just had one of the most powerful orgasms of his life, he'd be a fool to look down at that. He would just have to make it clear that that was a one time thing.

"And I still would like to accept your offer." With rosy cheeks, she reached into her purse and pulled out a pen to sign.

"Don't you want to read through it first?" He was mildly taken aback by her trust. It wasn't very wise, in a business sense.

"No need," she didn't look up. "Should anything go awry, I'm pretty sure I'll be adequately taken care of. Wouldn't you agree?"

Then she looked at him. And he knew right then and there she had him.

Nodding, he pursed his lips, "That I do." He reached for the divider switch and flicked it so it would go down. Apparently, they had been circling her block so it didn't take long to arrive at her place. Once the car was safely parked along the sidewalk, Adrien exited the car and reached in for her hand. She took it and was guided out into the warm night air.

"Thank you for an incredible end to my evening," she hummed.

"The thanks are all mine, believe me," he was shockingly still very much into this mystery woman and a part of him wanted to follow her inside and learn more about her. But, being bound by a signed contract, he knew that opportunity had passed. He grabbed her hand and kissed the top of it before she turned and walked toward her building. "I'll see you tomorrow at nine in the morning. The address is on your signed part of the paperwork."

"See you then," she smirked and entered her lock code into the door key pad. "And do try to control yourself, Adrien. Indiscretions no longer suit us."

Winking, she entered the foyer and he watched as she waved to the Bell man and disappeared into the elevator. Turning back to his car, he got in and shut the door. Making brief eye contact with his driver, who raised his eyebrows at him, Adrien noticed a piece of paper on the seat. Quickly grabbing it he noticed it was an old receipt. It was from...his heart sank into his stomach, Cafe Guerrab and the date was September 2002. The exact same time he had been there...

THE END

Chapter Seven

FROST BITING

So that's it?" Kara's, soon to be ex-husband asked while he watched her pack her suitcase. "You're just going to go sleep in a tent on one of the most dangerous mountains on the planet?"

"Seems so," she didn't look at him and pushed her backpack into her luggage before zipping it.

"First you tell me you need space, then you sell all our china on Craigslist, and now you're about to risk your life. You're only thirty-three for fuck's sake! Why do you want to risk your life? For what?"

He wasn't pleading, he was belittling. A man she once felt safe with, someone who would protect her and hold her heart with compassion and respect, had turned into a stranger shortly after tying the knot. And finally, three years later, Kara realized she deserved more. Never being that girl to grin and bear it, last week she made the decision to part ways when she realized at couple's therapy that there was simply no changing him. Nor did she want to change someone in order to be happy. She'd rather find happiness elsewhere. And, what better place than Alaska? Far from everything she'd ever known and loved, she hoped to find herself a renewed sense of life doing something that both scared and challenged her.

Finished with her packing, she stood and faced him to answer his patronizing question, "For everything."

...

Walking through the airport, Kara's heart began to race. Watching people walk past her, families and couples holding hands, she smiled at the future she had opened up for herself. Always loving the winter months, she's had this trip on her bucket list since jotting it down five years ago. Spending the last few months training at the local mountains with a club she had recently joined, she couldn't wait to meet up with them all again.

"Kara!" She heard a scream from the bar across from Gate 27.

"Eeeeek!" Kara squeaked when she spotted her new bff, Mary. Running over to her, she grinned from ear to ear when the rest of the group jumped from their seats to hug her.

"I can't believe the day is finally here!" Henry said, an older man, in his late fifties, she'd grown very close to. "I can't wait to see Tony in his pre-climb gear."

"You and me both," Courtney laughed and chugged her beverage.

"I wonder who the guides will be?" Kara asked the table.

"Well, we just met two of them right before you arrived. I heard they were the very best," Henry hummed. "Especially, Tony."

"You only saw him for three seconds," Katie quipped. "In his defense, he is pretty smokin'."

"Can I get you a drink?" A cute little blonde waitress asked Kara.

"I'll have a Bloody Mary, thank you," Kara answered and checked the time on her phone. "Where are they?"

"Who?" Mary asked.

"The guides," Kara took her jacket off and hung it on the chair behind her before sitting.

"They went to get forms they want us to fill out while we wait for the flight," Henry answered for her. "I think you'll fancy Tony's partner, Kara."

"Is that so?" Kara giggled. "I've only been single for five seconds."

"And?" Katie blurted.

Behind them, the two guides returned, one of them holding six clipboards. As they approached, Kara's coat fell from the chair. Noticing it, she stood and bent down to grab it when her hand was met with another's. It was strong and covered with a thin layer of dark hair and Kara felt sparks running up her arm. She raised her face to see the owner of such exquisite manliness and was met with the most hypnotic eyes she'd ever seen. Unable to swallow, she involuntarily moved her hand away from his and stood. He did the same.

"Thank you," she breathed. He was older, but not by much, and his features were dark and rugged.

"You're welcome," His Scottish accent nearly split her chest in two. He placed the boards on the table and hung her jacket back on her chair.

Kara couldn't speak and even if she could, she lacked the ability to formulate coherent thoughts. Desire rampaged through her body and when the waitress brought over her drink, she grabbed it and sucked it down faster than a plane's take-off speed. Listening to him talk to the two tables of climbers, she couldn't take her eyes off his lips and how she wanted to dig her teeth into them. Covered in a thin layer of dark hair, half of his face was hidden, but not his lips. She toyed with the straw in her glass with her tongue, hoping he'd look her way, but also hoping he didn't.

Get a hold of yourself, Kara. He could be married for all you know!

Just as she was about to break her trance, his eyes averted and landed right on her. Holding it for the exact amount of time needed to fill her imagination with enough ammunition to keep her warm during the frigid nights ahead.

"Kara?" Mary whispered with urgency.

"Yeah?" She snapped her head to her friend.

"Couldn't you hear me?" She examined Kara's face.

"Sorry, I was listening to what he was saying," she took the rest of her drink up through the straw. "I don't want to miss anything. What's up?"

"Um, did you see the way he looked at you just now?"

"Who?" Kara played dumb.

"That one," she nudged her head in the direction of the Scottish libido assailant. "It was intense."

"No, I must have missed it," she turned in her chair, away from him and back toward Mary.

She needed to regain some composure while the mystery man helped his partner hand out the forms and go over them at the other table. Trying to control the whirlwind of awakening prickling underneath her skin, she stopped breathing when Mary mouthed the words, 'he's coming'.

"Ladies," his words were like burning silk and melted over her senses, "and gentleman. I'm Cam and I'll be assigned to your safety for the foreseeable future. If you don't mind filling these out so we have any important medical information we may need."

"Didn't we already do this?" Henry asked in a flirty way. "I mean, it's not like we'll be summiting. This is a beginner adventure, correct?"

"Yes, I'm sure you did," Cam divvied up the pens, "but the system didn't send them over to me before I left this morning. And yes, it's a fairly easy trek. However, the latest weather report has suggested a bit of inhospitable conditions our second night in, and having all these filled out will give us an idea of any preexisting conditions that may make one more prone to hypothermia."

"Fair enough," Henry nodded and winked at him as he placed a board in front of each of them.

Standing breathtakingly too close to her, Kara smelled warm pine and wood coming from his body. Buzzing from the speech he just delivered, she felt herself moisten and questioned whether or not she was having a middle-life crisis. As they quietly filled out the one-page health survey, Kara couldn't help but steal glimpses of Cam while he drank a beer with his buddy at the bar. Deeply distracted by her sudden thirst, she basked in the renewed sense of fire she'd long been without. Just knowing she still had it in her was enough to make her come right there at the table and in front of everyone. She wondered if she'd ever get it back after the last few years of going unnoticed. Not knowing who this man was, she was already grateful for what he's managed to ignite in her with merely a glance and a faint touch.

Boarding the plane two hours later, Kara shoved her carry-on into the overhead compartment but she wasn't tall enough to get it in all the way. Standing on her tip-toes, two familiar hands pressed against the small luggage and pushed it all the way in for her. She looked up and her eyes met with Cam, who was looking down at her.

"Thank you," she breathed.

"We have to stop meeting like this," he winked and took his seat, which was directly where they were standing.

Kara looked at her ticket and quickly realized she would be sitting next to him for the entire flight. She wasn't sure if anyone else from her group would be in first class and was more than pleasantly surprised to have her companion be him. She blinked rapidly and inhaled before sitting next to him.

"Would you rather the window seat?" He asked with his far-off dialect and leaned toward her with his elbow on the seat rest.

"Oh, no I'm good here," she buckled up and he followed suit. All she could smell was him and it made her nipples hard. What the actual fuck is wrong with me? It's just a man. With typical man smell for God's sake.

"Excited?" He asked as he retrieved the beverage menu from the seat pocket in front of him. His jaw line was practically hypnotic to her and his voice certainly didn't help her relentless libido from twitching each time he spoke.

"Very much so," she wanted to look at him but knew that if she did, he'd know exactly all the wicked thoughts running through her mind. Trying to figure out why her lady bits were acting so unruly simply from the presence of this man, and why, whenever they made eye contact, she couldn't hear or see anything around them. It was as if time slowed whenever he looked at her and as much as she wanted to dive head-first into the enigma of him, she still maintained a fraction of sense. Knowing full well that this unorthodox behavior could have been manifested in her mind as a way of reminding her of the fact that she was now a single woman. Either way, she was torn. The force she felt when their eyes connected far outweighed the reasons to shy away but now being next to him for the next six hours, she wasn't sure what to do next.

"Apart from the questionable weather, which so far seems to be during the night hours, the rest of the journey should be exhilarating. Wait until you see the views, even from halfway." He reached down into his carry-on and pulled out a book titled High Altitude Exploration.

"I hope my gear is good enough for the storm," Kara spoke softly, hoping to minimize the odds of him noticing her ravenous attraction to him.

"You purchased the brands and weights as suggested on the prep sheet, right?" He seemed highly concerned, which made her heart skip a beat.

"I did," she looked over at him with the intent on doing so quickly, but the moment his caramel eyes connected with hers, she was left in a trance that only being bumped in to by a passenger loading her luggage in the overhead compartment above her could severe. "The only issue is my gloves. They were out of stock of the Mountain Hardware so I went with the Eddie Bauer."

She could feel his eyes on her, and it took all she could muster to not melt in front of him. "You should be alright. I'll be with you the entire time."

She turned and looked at him.

"You let me know if you start feeling anything funny."

"Will do," She couldn't peel herself away from him, but Mary's piercing voice got to her back into reality.

"Kara!"

Kara turned her head toward the aisle and looked back a few rows. Mary was in the last row of first-class, waving obnoxiously at her. She smiled at Mary and mouthed, 'you're in first class too!' To which Mary nodded. Kara gave her a thumbs up and went to turn back around but paused when Mary started making goo-goo eyes at her travel companion. Kara smiled and shook her head to play off the tease, even though Mary wasn't wrong. There was something enigmatic about him and a large part of her hoped to find out what exactly that was.

"Can I offer either of you a drink?" The stewardess addressed the two of them, keeping her eyes on Cam.

"What would you like," he spoke softly to Kara, leaning in close to her.

"I don't know if I should," she whispered out of the corner of her mouth. "The Bloody Mary seems to have a hold on me."

"So, you like Vodka?" He asked, apparently not concerned with her current state.

"Like is a strong word," she giggled.

"We'll take two vodka cranberries," he ordered for them both. "Extra vodka."

"Well, alrighty then," she said to no one and laughed. "A drink it is!"

Two hours into the flight, and after loads of indisputable flirting between the two, Kara had dozed off. Being completely unaware that her head was resting on Cam's shoulder, her eyes jolted open when the attendant came around with snacks. Frozen in place while she tried to make sense of her surroundings, she slowly lifted her head from him. Keeping her body in place, she tilted herself into him.

"I am so sorry," she whispered. "Why didn't you nudge me?"

"Because," he answered with an unspoken message she longed to unravel.

Sitting up, she checked the time on her phone. His knee was touching hers and she wondered if he noticed. "One hour left."

The rest of the flight was mostly uneventful. Cam was bust filling out some forms and Kara had finished half of her romance novel. Having their legs practically touching most of the trip, she noticed the muscles he had inside them tested the durability of the fabric. This man was powerful. Strong, and riddled with an endurance that sent shivers down her spine. She couldn't help but steal glances of his crotch in the hopes of it somehow manifesting it to make it's way into her tent later.

They landed at 5pm and the group decided to go out for a nice dinner before embarking on the first stretch early tomorrow morning. Knowing they would have sunlight for most of the time, making sure they had a good night's sleep was imperative.

Kara sat with Mary, Katie, and Henry at one end of the table while the others, along with Cam and Tony, sat across from them. Throughout the meal, laughter and information were shared and in between speakers, Kara caught Cam looking at her more times than she could count. Filling with heat, she needed to get to her room for a cold shower so her wits would hopefully return. However, fighting the intense urge to sneak into his room later would be a test of her will that luckily, was governed by tomorrow's requirement of a rested body. She sighed internally and happened upon the plan of simply satisfy herself and calling it a night. As she did most nights. And even though the booze warming her veins taunted her to go after what she wanted, she didn't want to come off a certain way. Despite the fact that Cam's lips seemed to be calling her her through his dark, close-cut, beard.

Once the bill was paid, the group stood and said their good nights before heading to their rooms. She was happy to be bunking with Katie because being alone would not be conducive to her plan of being responsible.

"Good night, Kara," he said from behind her, causing her to whip around.

"Same to you," her tone was silky and inviting, and one he could not mistake as enticing.

He smiled and went on his way, as did she.

The morning came fast but Kara felt oddly refreshed, mostly having to do with the adrenaline filling her veins. Not saying much to one another, they all showered, packed, and ate breakfast before heading for the transport shuttle.

Kara only saw Cam for a few minutes at breakfast as they were at separate tables. However, even during that short time, he managed to make her feel giddy and excited with just a glance. It was an immediate attraction that ran deep within her and she was pretty sure at this point, he felt the same. The eye contact had only increased and each time it happened, it lasted longer than the time before. Smiling before resuming what they had been doing, the two definitely had some chemicals in the Bunsen burner.

The ride to the base of Squak Glacier was fast, landing them unloaded and ready to ascend by 7am. By the time everyone had their gear on, Cam and Tony gave them the run through. Kara managed to keep a serious demeanor during that time because, despite the fun it was to feel her crotch tingle, she didn't feel like dying this week. However, when the talk wrapped up, a part of her wanted to barrel through the group and slam him down into the snow to hump the hell out of him. I'm a pleasure-seeking slut goddamn it! Hear me roar!

Tony led them on their way and Cam kept up the rear. His backpack was enormous compared to everyone else's and Kara made sure she slowed to enter the line in order to be closer to him. As luck would have it, he was directly behind her.

"How long have you been guiding people?" She turned her head and glanced at him. The trail was relatively moderate and so far, shockingly doable.

"Going on thirteen years this October."

"Wow! You must love it out here."

"I do," his voice turned poetic. "It's the only place I feel I'm doing something right."

"Is that so?"

"It is," he answered matter-of-factly.

She let her mind wander off, keeping his last comment the driving force of her daydream. Wondering what he'd be like with her body in his hands. Would he be rough? Would he take his time? Would he be unable to control himself long enough to take her to the edge more than once? All of the above? With the air being colder than she had ever imagined, she was really hoping for all of the above just to warm her up.

"What brings you all the way out here...on your own," the hum of his words shot right through her back and webbed across her stomach, latching on to her primal urges and stimulating the deepest parts of her awakening.

"It was time for a change," Kara answered, suddenly realizing her hands were tingling. Shaking them, she continued. "I'm in the beginning stages of a divorce. Staying home is too awkward at the moment and I felt like if I didn't get out and do something wild and out of character, I'd never leave."

"Why do you think you'd never leave?" He was closer to her now, she could feel his presence only a couple of feet back. Opposed to the many that had spaced them apart earlier.

"Because I'd let the guilt consume me until it changed my mind. What about you? Is there anyone you leave at home when you come out here?" She hoped that was alright to ask. It was the last bit of information she needed before a decision could be made to either keep it casual or go full-on flirt mode. The latter being more enticing. However, she was starting to feel off and her body was shivering for a different reason. The weather had been mild when they first embarked, but the wind gusts brought a chill that seemed to not want to leave her.

"You doing alright up there?" He yelled through the wind cyclone that engulfed the group.

"Yeah," she yelled back, "I'm just really cold. Oddly cold."

The next thing she knew, she heard a beep and Cam talking to someone, "Tony, head right to the ridge at Cross Canyon. It should only take us about five minutes to reach. We need to set up the tents before the weather worsens. Looks like the storm has arrived earlier than expected."

She followed in line until they reached the spot to rest. Katie and Mary bounced over to her and they three bobbed up and down in a huddle while the shelters were assembled. They were brilliant designs and each double occupancy enclosure unfolded and whipped into its shape within seconds. Lined along a small tree line that overlooked a massive expansion of Earth, the three looked out over the cliff at the view.

"At least the sun won't fully set. I'd freak the fuck out being out here in the pitch black," Katie worried and rubbed her gloved hands together. "I just want to lay down and disappear into my sleeping bag. I'm so fucking cold."

Kara didn't say much. She was finding it hard to understand her friend's words and knew that if she didn't sit soon, she would quite possibly fall over. She didn't notice others experiencing the same level of discomfort as she was and that concerned her. She had read about different health issues one could obtain on such an extreme trip but figured she had dressed warm enough to avoid those things.

"Holy shit," Mary checked her watch, "It's negative twenty degrees!"

Being fully masked and covered, Kara turned toward the men and saw that her tent was ready to be loaded. Tapping Mary on the back, the two went to set up their beds while Katie and the others did the same.

Once her gear was set up, Kara tucked herself in without saying good night to the group. The wind had died down an hour ago, and the fire could be seen through the canvas of her tent. Unable to sleep, Kara shivered in the same clothes she wore all day until the zipper lifted.

"Hey," Mary whispered, "you alright? Did you eat what I gave you?"

"Yes," Kara answered, her voice chattering. "I don't feel well. Like I'm going in slow motion."

The next thing Kara heard was the zipper returning to the bottom. Lifting her head, which was now shaking, she saw Mary's silhouette walking back toward the fire and stopping in front of someone. When they stood, she could tell it was a man by his size and after a few moments, he began walking in her direction. The zipper lifted.

"Kara," it was him.

"Hey, Cam," she tried to appear normal but failed.

"You need to come with me," he opened the door fully.

"I don't think I can move," she was getting scared.

"You're experiencing pre-hypothermia," he crawled inside her tent and tucked his arms under her. "You don't need to move."

"Wait," she tried to get up on her own but couldn't. "You can't carry me out, it's too cold out there."

"I'm taking you into my tent. I have special equipment and strategies that will make you feel better. If we don't, you could take a turn for the worse. Having asthma leaves you at a higher susceptibility of this."

She didn't fight him. Lifting her against his body, sleeping bag and all, he managed to get them out and over to his. "She's not doing well, Tony. I need to warm her up immediately."

"Let me know if you need extra heating pads," Tony yelled over the flames to Cam.

Katie got up and ran to Cam's tent to unzip it for him so he wouldn't have to put her down. "Thank you, Katie."

Once inside, she re-zipped it and left them alone. He placed her gently on the far side of the space so he could unzip his sleeping bag. "Now, it's going to be tight in here, but we need to get in together."

Kara turned to her side and watched as he started to remove his clothing. Am I dreaming right now? Through her blurred vision, she could see his chest was covered in tattoos. As well as his arms. Leaving his boxers on, he went over to Kara and undid her bag.

"We need to get your clothes off," his tone didn't sound light. He was frantic and also beginning to freeze. She tried to help him but her fingers were too stiff. "And we need to do it quick."

With the fire blazing outside, she remained motionless as he undid her jacket. Quickly, and without any hidden meaning. Helping her out of it, he draped it over her while he addressed her pants and boots. Making quick work of her laces, he took each one off and removed the damp and from her frozen feet. Without meaning to, he ran his hands up the sides of her legs before reaching the top of her pants to remove them. It was quiet in the tent. Only their breathing and the sounds of clothes being removed could be heard over the snapping of the fire outside.

Tugging her pants until they were off, he tried to avert his eyes from looking at her in her underwear. Lifting her shirt over her head was the last step and once her hair fell free from it, he picked her up and placed her inside his sleeping bag. Grabbing his two-way radio, he positioned himself on his side next to her before zipping them in. Her feet were ice-cold and he placed his calves beside them to warm them up. Their legs tangled and he wrapped his arms around her in a spoon position. Her body trembled and he tried to slow his breathing in order to release his body heat onto her.

Her mind was racing and she couldn't tame it. She felt drunk and on the verge of passing out and if it wasn't for the fact that she was aware of how close they were, she very well may have.

"Shhhh," he held her tight to him and whispered into her ear, "try and relax your muscles and let my warmth enter you. You're too tense."

She tried focusing on her breathing. She could feel the hair on his chest against her back, and his strong legs curled up with hers. Grabbing each of her hands in his, he closed himself around her even more. Bringing his knees up and making hers follow. His breathing made her hair move back and forth across her forehead, warming her exposed face.

"Good girl," he hummed as her shivers lessened. "Feel my heat."

She wasn't sure if he was trying to sound sexual or if he was simply gifted with unknowing sensuality. All she did know was that her clarity was returning and her body was well aware of what was pressed up against it. Without meaning to, and having the words 'good girl' floating around in her mind, she tucked into him with a slight sway of her body. Trying, but not to forwardly, to rub her ass into him. Which just so happened to fall exactly where she had hoped.

"Woah, careful," he choked on his words and adjusted his hips so he wouldn't be pressing into her as he felt himself begin to thicken. "Sorry, the curse of the male."

"Thank you, for doing this. For saving my life." Her voice was steadier as her body temperature continued to rise.

"It's a debt I'm willing to pay," he talked softly. "I need you to turn over so we can warm the front of you now."

Her eyes popped open at the thought of her seeing his face combined with their flesh touching. This ought to be interesting. Her clit throbbed when he used his arms to turn her toward him. A delicate maneuvering filled with heavy breathing and tension. Unsure of where to place her legs in this new position, he took charge and wrapped one of her legs above his hip and the other between his thighs before bringing her fully into him. He kept his body still so her body could stop shaking.

"There you go," he had one of his hands on her back and the other behind her head cupping it into his neck.

She could feel his dick pulse between her legs, despite him trying to hide it by pulling back a little. She knew he needed to be professional and couldn't be so forward and inappropriate with a customer. However, there was something undeniable between them that she had felt when first laying eyes on him and no matter how hard she knew this wasn't the time or place, she figured this was the perfect time and place. Unable to hide her hunger for him, the tendons surrounding her pussy clenched. Giving his dick an unsolicited squeeze.

"Don't do that," he gripped her hair in his hand. It happened again of its own accord. He caught his breath and closed his eyes. "Don't."

"I suppose it's the curse of the female," she quipped him back with his own reasoning. Having her hands curled up between their stomachs, she had an idea. "Can you undo my bra?"

"What?" He could barely speak.

"I feel I'd warm up faster if it was off," she explained.

He gulped but didn't argue. Keeping his fist tight in her hair, he used his one hand to unclasp her bra. Once it was freed, he slowly dragged down the strap from her arm. Letting his fingers run along her skin. She exhaled and swayed her hips.

"Careful," he pleaded. "Don't, breath like that."

"I can't help it," her head was spinning. She was so cold and also so aroused she didn't know which way was up. All she did know was that she wanted him to touch her more. "It just feels so good, the way you, do things."

"Kara," his length grew in his boxers and between her legs and she moaned. Returning to her ear, he spoke quietly enough for her to hear, "you're very responsive. That's a good sign."

Her head fell heavy onto his arm, exposing her neck to him. She could feel him breathe against her cheek and longed for him to touch his lips to her skin. Her breathing increased and her leg muscles twitched. Then she heard the walkie-talkie flick on again.

"Tony," Cam's voice was heavy.

"Yeah, Cam?"

"Before I left the fire, I put an extra pair of gloves on the ridge to warm them. Can you bring them to the tent door?"

"Roger that." Within a few seconds, Tony was at the zipper.

"Just toss them in," Cam instructed. "We are still in the sleeping bag."

"It's that bad, huh?" He did as Cam asked and sealed it back up. "He'll get the job done, Kara. Don't you worry. Just let the man do his thing."

Oh, I'm gonna let him. Unsure of why he'd want a pair of gloves at a time like this, but she figured she was about to find out. Having caught them with his one hand, still holding her head with the other, he brought them into the sleeping bag. Looking up at him, her vision had returned. She watched his face change from survival-mode to something much more primitive and thirsty. Tilting his body into her, he moved her onto her back and took one of the heated gloves. Significantly cooled from the frigid air, the temperature was still enough to make her gasp when he placed it between her breasts and began to trail it down her stomach. An explosion of passion and warmth consumed her. She arched her back as he brought the fingers of the mitt tantalizingly close to her panties, hovering over her lower stomach.

She quivered beneath his work even though she couldn't see what he was doing. Bringing the glove back up her core, he brought it to the center of her exposed breasts and lightly grazed the crest of them with the fabric. He watched in the dim light as her nipple hardened.

"So very responsive," he breathed close to her face, his mouth inches from hers.

"What is this?" She opened her eyes and looked at him, melting even further into him.

"I don't know," he fought to stay in control, "but it's definitely something."

Leaning down as if to kiss her, he derailed and ran his cheek down hers until his breath filled her eardrum. Her body slithered as he continued to warm her breasts, all the while holding his fist tightly in place within her hair. As if to control her.

"I like watching you squirm," he spoke poetically and dropped the glove to use his hand instead. "I've never desired a woman as much as I desire you."

She gasped when his finger made contact with her puckered flesh. Swirling her nipple in between his fingers, he moved his dick to stimulate her already growing nerve. He watched her intently, his eyes going dark with need and lust. Touching her lobe with his tongue, she let out all the air in her lungs and tightened her leg around him. Lifting his head while keeping their faces touching, he paused when their lips were seconds apart from touching. Both panting and wanting this to linger, their attempts to connect were subtle yet filled with unimaginable need. Releasing her breast, his hand trailed down her body until hooking underneath her underwear.

"Cam," she opened her legs for him, "save me."

"I intend to," he let his fingers slither under the fabric holding her captive and watched her face morph into ecstasy when he reached her clit.

His lower lip touched hers but he didn't kiss her and she almost came right then and there. Trying to lift her head to further the sensations his mouth was giving her while his hand explored every fold and nerve between her legs, he remained in control.

"You're so smooth," he continued to massage and flick every sensitive part between her legs until he could feel her heat surrounding his hand. Rubbing her moisture all over her pleading pussy and outer lips, his breathing started to become labored.

"I think it's...working," she writhed under his hand and let her tongue slither out of her mouth to touch his lip. His head shook with temptation as Kara continued to taste him, fueling his senses with urgency.

Pausing his finger assault, but keeping his hand in place, he looked Kara in the eyes and tilted his head ever so slightly. Knowing he was about to kiss her, she parted her lips and lifted her chin to meet him half way. When all four made contact, he let out a small whimper before deepening the pressure. Keeping their movements barely noticeable, they relished in the feel of each other. He let out his tongue enough to grace the tip of hers and resumed playing with her between her legs. The combination of his mouth and fingers sent her into a state of entrancement and she couldn't do anything besides lay still and let him have his way with her. Every inch of her body trembled and he could feel on his hand that she was close.

"You know," he spoke into her mouth, keeping his lip on hers, "frost bite is very dangerous. It can eat you alive."

"Can it?" Her chest lifted off the sleeping pad when he plunged two of his fingers inside of her. She let out a soft scream that he muffled with his mouth.

"It can," he growled, "but not unless I eat you first."

Biting her lower lip, he let his fingers slide out her so he could unzip the sleeping bag. Reaching for his gear, he grabbed a thermal blanket from his pack and tossed it on top of him as he slithered his way down her body, inhaling every inch of her on his way. Her toes curled when his warm breath spread over her soaked pussy. Closing her eyes, she savored the way he moved his nose against her clit, tenderly letting her know he was about to take good care of her. The underside of his tongue landed on top of her sensitive button and pressed down until the tip of it was at her entrance. She moaned and grabbed the sleeping bag in her hands as he buried the thickness of it deep inside of her. Tasting her and coaxing her back to the edge by curling it up toward her g-spot.

Her breathing was rapid and she had to wrap her legs around the back of him in order to ground herself. Grinding his mouth against her clit, he continued to penetrate her with his long and thirsty muscle until her walls began to twitch around it. He hummed into her, ready for whatever she was willing to offer him.

"Oh my God," she choked out the words as her nerve pounded with intensity. Trapping him inside of her as she clenched down on him, he continued to flick her spot until she opened up and let it wash over him. She made a guttural sound every ounce of gratification coated his face.

He drank and sucked from her until her body relaxed and floated back down onto his hands. Hard as a rock, he crawled his way back out of the sleeping bag, stopping when the tip of his dick was at the gate he just savored. Treating it with warm moisture, he pulled both of her knees out to the side as far as the sleeping bag would allow.

"I need to open you up," he growled. She licked her lips while staring at his, still wet from her orgasm. "Can you do that?"

"Yes," she pleaded. "Do whatever you want to me."

"Be careful what you say, beautiful," he panted and pushed forward enough to allow half of his head to enter her.

She let out a moan and he covered her mouth with his hand while using his other to grasp under her ass. Using his arm muscles, he pressed her tightly against him and stopped when the ridge of his tip was submerged into her tight opening.

"I knew the second I touched your hand that I would need to feel what it's like to be inside you," he pushed himself in a little more. Closing his eyes. She squeezed her walls around his cock, taunting him to slam his entire length into her. "When you looked at me, my insides unraveled. And they haven't been the same since."

"Deeper," she begged, "I want to connect fully with you."

"I fear I won't be able to stop once I start," he warned, almost halfway inside her.

"Good," she panted, digging her nails into his ass and trying to push him in deeper.

"Greedy little minx," he bit her lower lip before kissing her, continuing to get lost within her. "I want you to take from me. Take everything you need."

"I need you to fuck me," her eyes flung open and she rammed her hips up to engulf herself around his entirety.

"Oh fuck!" He grunted and remained still as she slammed herself up and down his shaft. Massaging thickness with her grip. "Fuck."

"I knew you'd feel this good," she dug her heels into his hamstrings for support.

"Roll over for me," he pulled out of her and she whimpered, doing as he wished.

Caressing her ass with his hands, he leaned forward and let his dick slide between her cheeks. The friction against her asshole made her eyes roll back in her head and as if he knew what he was doing to her, he reached one of his hands underneath her until landing on her swollen nerve. With his body weight on top of her, he positioned himself to enter her from behind. Tilting her hips to receive him, she yelled into the sleeping bag's fluffy material when he filled her with one thrust. His size stretched her the perfect amount and the natural curve of his cock collided with her spot with each plunge he took.

"What do I feel like," he whispered in her ear while fucking her slowly.

"You feel incredible," she turned her head to the side. "Like an avalanche waiting to destroy me."

Picking up his rhythm, his ass rose and fell until his nuts coiled. Rubbing her clit with force, her legs began to vibrate which was all it took for him to explode into her.

"Fuck!" He bit her neck and let every thought he had created of her in his mind pour out of him. He kissed her while her head was turned, keeping his dick in place. Swerving his pelvis forward and backward to pump himself in their fluids. "Let me warm you from the inside. Come for me."

Gripping her throat with his other hand and cradling it while he nibbled her ear, he increased his speed. "Harder!"

He did as she demanded and pounded her into the bed mat. His fingers never wavering from their play, her entire body quivered until the friction from their sexes brought her to release. Screaming into hands, she collapsed around him. Shaking violently as he softened his finger play in order to prolong her pleasure.

"Oh my...God," she continued to twitch and curl up and he continued to deliver whatever he could to ensure her depletion. Lowering his hand from her neck to caress her breast, he gently pinched her nipple until he was covered in her wet heat.

When her body stilled, he let himself fall out of her and rolled her onto her back to face him. They looked into each others' eyes and as he was about to speak, the walkie-talkie beeped on.

"Cam?" Tony sounded concerned.

Cam reached out of the sleeping bag and grabbed the device, pressing himself against her sex. She moaned and wiggled under him. "Yeah," he answered, out of breath.

"We heard a cry or something and wanted to make sure she was okay in there. Need anything?"

"No, sorry," Cam put on his act, "When I was zipping up the sleeping bag, I accidentally snagged her hair."

"Roger that," Tony believed him, "How's she doing?"

"I think she'll live," his deep voice vibrated through her bones.

"Good, because the storm is coming," she could hear shuffling on his end, "we are all going to bunker down until it ends. May be a while."

"Understood," Cam was calm, which made her relax instead of panic.

He tossed it to the side and returned to her. "How are you feeling now?"

"I feel right as rain," she purred. "But I am not sure I'll be able to climb tomorrow after that."

"Well good news," he gave her a long peck on the lips, "No one will be hiking tomorrow. So we will have plenty of time to ensure your body temperature remains stable."

"Well," she dug her nails into his back, "feel like pulling an all nighter?"

"Absofuckinglutely I do," and he slammed his mouth into hers, continuing to share the small space for the next fourteen hours while waiting for their evacuation team to arrive.

Knowing how Cam made her feel, and how she made him unhinged, there was no doubt in her mind that this wouldn't be the last time she'd be with this man. And the way he was kissing her as the fire outside dwindled, she smiled at the realization he'd never let her go.

To be continued...

Chapter Eight

CONTRITION

PART ONE

I n the name of the Father, the Son, and of the Holy Spirit, it's been twenty-seven years since..." Trista paused and turned her eyes toward the mesh barrier between herself and the Priest. Having never been to confessional, or mass for that matter, all she knew to do was what she had googled before arriving.

"Go on," he whispered. His voice was deep and rattled the decorative metal holding the screen in place.

"The truth is," she began, shaky and already embarrassed, "I've never been inside of a church. I feel that's important to start with."

He said nothing.

"Maybe it's not. It's just that my family wasn't really in to the whole 'religion' thing and I...," crap that was so rude. This guy gave up his life for this and I just air quoted the very basis of his existence. Smooth. "I've always wanted to be a part of something bigger than myself."

"There is no need for you to explain your past to me. We are both here in the present and for one singular reason. If you are here to repent for something you feel goes against your moral compass, I find it's best to keep the minor details out of the limelight and to keep your focus on what's really troubling you."

Trista was mortified. She went in to this unsure, and with a certain level of anxiety, at the thought of actually saying what she had to say out loud. But when he spoke, the rattling in her core seemed to subside a little, which she had been praying for since the incident. The quiet that now surrounded her lungs made it easier for her to breathe. She wondered if this momentary relief in guilt was the main reason people came to confession, leaving penance a secondary perk.

"Right," she swallowed and prepared herself for the delivery of the greatest shame of her life, thus far. "Best get on with it then. I slept with my Mother's new boyfriend's son, Tim."

Silence.

Oh God I'm going to hell.

"You see, when he came over last weekend, as he does every weekend, he brought his son with him. It was the first time meeting him and everything was perfectly normal and ordinary. He's only a few years younger than me but once the drinking started, he began acting...with intent, so to speak. I've been single for longer than I care to admit, but I will if that's part of the deal here!"

"Only tell me what you need to," he was so monotone and nonjudgemental. This is wonderful!

"You got it. Where was I? Oh yeah, being single for as far back as I can remember made his advances turn me quite giddy. And, long story short, one thing led to another, and...yeah."

Silence.

"That's all, Father," she had nothing else to admit and already felt better getting it out. Even her closest friends had no idea she had suddenly, and without warning, turned into a hussy. I can never go home again!

"What is it you wish to take away from this? What are you seeking penance for?" The tone of his voice resonated in her stomach. Each time he spoke, she could feel the wood around her vibrate. I think he may have the deepest voice I've ever heard. Wild.

"Um," what did she hope to get out of this? Forgiveness? Reassurance that her actions wouldn't tear apart her mother's new relationship? A relationship she knew her mother didn't take lightly, considering her father had only passed away less than a year ago. "I guess I'm hoping my mother isn't crushed by our actions. I don't know if it's best to come clean or to hope she never finds out. I can handle the consequences but I can't handle if she feels betrayed by me."

"Why would she feel betrayed? You were with his son, not him. Correct?" He sounded less like a priest and more like a neighbor she'd shoot the shit with.

"Yes, but," she wanted to explain herself but was struggling with finding the words.

"How did being with him make you feel?" He asked, throwing her for a loop. What the heck does he mean by that? Like, how did the sex make me feel? Or how did I feel afterwards?

"Being with him was exciting," her fingers were fidgety as she recounted the scandalous scene in her head. "Being touched, after having not been for so long was, too hard for me to shut down. It was as if he'd been without human contact for years and used my body as a way of remembering. The way his finger slid down my spine so softly, it was like he was exploring every bump and crevice of my vertebrae. I didn't even see him coming. I was in the garage grabbing another bottle of wine for my mother and before I closed the fridge, that's when I felt it."

She shifted on the bench in the hopes of taming the arousal that was now culminating between her legs as she recalled the accounts of that night. And even in knowing this was hardly appropriate banter to be having with a man of God, she couldn't stop.

"We were about to go into the hot tub, and I was in my bikini. Which certainly didn't help matters, but I played along. It was fun and innocent until that finger made contact with me. I couldn't turn around to face him. I was nervous but also ready to do... whatever."

The priest cleared his throat and swallowed. Great Trista, you're making him uncomfortable. But could she stop? No.

"The combination of booze and deprivation resulted in a whirlwind of untamed reactions. Things started pulsing that hadn't pulsed in a long time. If you know what I mean."

Shit! Did I really just say that? "Sorry, is this too much?"

"It's whatever you need to say," his voice seemed more restricted than before, but she paid little attention to that as her story was getting her all hot and bothered. Sharing only seemed fair.

I'm going to hell. Maybe I'm going through a mid-life crisis!

"I knew my mother and Keith, her boyfriend, had already gone into the hot tub while I had gone upstairs to get my suit on, and assumed Tim had joined them. But, he hadn't. I can still feel his touch going lower and lower down my back, hooking into the bottom of my bathing suit. That's when I felt the warmth of his breath on my neck. 'There is something about you,' he had whispered. My hair was up in a clip, so each word he spoke penetrated my flesh and swirled all the way down between my legs."

That was probably a little TMI.

She looked up and noticed the priest had changed from an upright position to a slightly hunched forward one. Although the open square between them was difficult to see through, in the shadows she could tell he was getting antsy. Maybe I'm taking too long.

"I'm sorry, I'm sure I'm out of time and you have mass to prepare for." She stated, still feeling the effects of her story.

"No," he said abruptly, which startled her. "Excuse me, I meant to say that there is no mass scheduled this evening and when you are through, I will go. So there is no rush. If you'd like to continue."

"I think I've said enough," she whispered, wanting very badly to go home and fantasize about that night. "Do you have any prayers I can say to maybe erase what I've done?"

She forced her legs together in the hope to ease the need growing between her legs, trying to use the movements to temporarily entertain the itch. Even knowing how wrong it was to fuck him, and how he must have formed certain assumptions about her afterward, it didn't prevent the memories of how he had claimed her from washing over her, repeatedly. She needed to find a distraction. And fast. The sound of a door closing snapped her out of her thoughts. She recalled the church being empty when she arrived a little bit ago, being so late in the evening. She looked up and noticed that the priest's silhouette was no longer there.

"What the h..." she started to stand, but the door to her chamber opened so quickly, she stumbled back onto the bench.

Her eyes blossomed wildly at the sight of him. The Priest. The one she had just confessed, and in great detail, how her deprived body made poor judgement calls. His eyes were dark and burned right into her. She swallowed, nervous and stimulated. What is happening? Was this a customary way of escorting a sinner into the pit of hell?

"Forgive me," he spoke with an audible thirst that made her pussy flutter, "but I seem to have lost my will. You must go."

"Go?" She was horrified.

"Now," He nodded while white knuckling the doorframe, which she noticed. She grabbed her purse and stood quickly. He didn't move. They stared at each other, both unsure of how to move. He was more rugged than she'd expect from a priest. Lean and muscular with the aroma of a lumberjack or woodsman. Silver streaks ran through his clean-cut hair which made her question why she had never been with an older man. The sheer dominance he exuded was other-worldly, godly even. Suddenly, she felt like a school-girl standing in front of a hot Science teacher. Or, a twenty-seven-year old standing in front of the sexiest man she's ever seen. Either worked. Once again, filling her mind with naughty doings that she should know better than to have.

"Excuse me," she nodded and stepped toward the door, but he didn't budge. She was only inches from him now and involuntarily reached her hand up to his chest, but froze before making contact. His hand only squeezed harder. Why do I want him to touch me so badly?

"Forgive me, Father," he took a step toward her, forcing his body into her hand, and inside the chamber, "for I am about to sin."

Holy Shit. Her nipples instantly hardened and her eyes widened as he reached his arm behind him to close the door, never taking his gaze off of her. With a twist of his fingers, he latched the lock. She tried to swallow the lump in her throat at the thought of what was about to happen. He practically filled the small space with his massive build, and had a wild look in his eyes that no one in his position should have. She could feel the sexual hunger emitting from him as it surrounded her trembling body. The arousal from her story had momentarily faded into an internal struggle of nervousness and anticipation. Not knowing what to expect from a man much older than her, she quickly realized that this may be just what she needed to forget what had happened the other night. Do two sins make a right?

She couldn't speak, nor did she want to. He was close enough now for her to feel the heat coming from him and it warmed her shivering flesh. His upper lip twitched as he examined her. She could tell he was hesitant, but also, that he wasn't about to let that stop him. Out of nowhere, he fell forward. Slamming both of his hands against the ornate wood behind her and causing her to, once again, lower back on to the bench.

He closed his eyes and exhaled before looking down at her. Her body was still, apart from the pounding in her chest. I suppose a heart attack in the house of God is a good way to go. Just then, with his right arm, he bent down and slowly wrapped it around her waist before lifting her. Inch by inch she got closer to his face, their bodies connecting like silk in the wind. He was unsuitably handsome and brought out a certain obedience in her as if she had no choice in the matter, but was also not fighting it.

With their faces only inches apart, he rubbed his cheek against hers and inhaled deeply. Her knees weakened but in the strength of his arm, she didn't wither. She clung to the desire of being touched by him and knew she would be. The heat between their bodies erased all her apprehension and she let out a sigh of pleasure. This only fueled his advances and shattered what little control he had left. With his other hand pressed firmly against the wall behind them, he swayed his hips forward and gently grazed his shaft between her legs. With as little force as possible, he explored what it felt like to be this close to a woman. To have his most intimate place touch another's was forever a forbidden act, and tonight, he was willing to throw that all out the proverbial creed window.

"Be still," he panted as he massaged himself against her awakened pussy.

She tried her hardest to do as he instructed, not moving and allowing him to bring her to a place her body desperately needed. She could barely maintain the onslaught of arousal that coursed through her veins and allowed him to obtain whatever pleasure he sought from her. Wondering if he'd take it to higher levels, her hips began to move of their own accord. This started a frenzy he could no longer inhibit, despite having voiced to her to remain still. His body froze from the over-stimulation she was now bestowing upon him, allowing her to move as she needed and absorbing all the sensations that came along with it. She could feel the blood rushing through his cock as she rubbed her nerve against it in a slow dance of temptation. The thrill of being with someone off limits was too hard to resist and combating their primitive urges was proving difficult.

He clamped his teeth on her exposed neck in the hopes of regaining a handle on the situation but she let out a groan that sent his pulse racing. Still draped over his arm, he took his other arm and grabbed hold of her hair. He was as hard as a rock and pressed it further into her from under his robe. Her leggings were saturated from the unthinkable acts they were doing in the house of God, but breaking this momentum was no longer on the table. This is what priests do...they take you to Heaven's gate. She was a sinner, and for the time being, accepted her fate as such.

With parted lips, he grazed her's ever so delicately. Thousands of electrical explosions erupted with each tender connection the silky skin made, their tongues only a hairline away from touching. She whimpered under his caress and into his mouth to which he could not properly contain himself any longer.

Wrapping both of his arms tightly around her and squeezing her into him, their mouths slammed together, shattering all hope of restraint.

A barely audible 'fuck' escaped his mouth when he moved his hands lower and clutched her ass in his large, deprived hands. He continued to grind his raging cock against her clit as a whirlwind of ecstasy began culminating between her legs. His moves were deliberate and amazingly accurate. He pulled back a little in order to rub only the tip of him under the folds of her moist lips. *These clothes are in the way...*

She decided to go full on devil and grabbed one of his hands from her ass and guide it into the back of her pants. He didn't complain and trailed his palm down and under her peach, inches away from her entrance. *Oh God, touch me!* The stubble on his face burned her delicate skin as their mouths continued to dance frantically. He tightened the grip on her flesh and growled when her moisture glazed his fingers. *I'm going to come. Shit.* But he pulled away. Leaving them panting and staring at each other.

The look of turmoil and passion painted his face as he struggled to regain composure. She, on the other hand, wanted none of that. She walked toward him, and he stepped back. Crashing into the door behind him. She bit her lip and reached up to undo the clasp that held his robe closed. He didn't stop her. When it was undone, she watched as it slowly fell to the floor. Leaving him fully exposed. He was naked under there! She looked down at his dick and almost fainted. The combination of natural instinct laced with the unspoken taboo acts they had already committed was almost too much for her to handle. All she knew, was that she needed that cock inside of her immediately, and he wanted the same.

He didn't fight it when she turned their positions around, making it his turn to sit on the bench. Naked, and undeniably ready. His jaws clenched as she slowly lowered her leggings, making sure to leave her thong on. Both of his hands twitched and his mouth dampened at the sight of her. She walked to him and slowly lifted one of her legs onto the seat, opening herself up right in front of him. He looked down at her soft bulge hiding behind her panties and licked his lips. Trailing one of his hands up her standing leg, her skin broke out in goosebumps as he approached her center. Careful not to miss a single reaction from her, he watched her face as his fingers tenderly brushed along her sex. He lowered his body so his mouth was level with her mound and moved the skimpy fabric over to reveal her plump, wet lips.

His breathing halted at the sight. It was something he's never seen in person, but now wanted a taste. To experience the essence of life on his tongue from a woman was something he'd never dared think about, but often dreamed of. And now here it was, right in front of him and close enough to smell. He held on to her ass with his free hand, while keeping the material out of the way. Her folds were smooth and glistened in the candlelight and he knew this would be the end of him. Burying his nose in the fabric of her underwear, he inhaled harder than he ever had before and had to brace himself with his free hand from the heavenly gratification. She watched him toy with her as he explored all she had to offer. His tongue touched her first and she had to hold on to the walls on either side of her in order not to fall over. She had been close to coming moments ago and knew it would only take one touch to undo her. He growled like a lion as he circled her nerve with painstakingly deliberate aim. Holy shit...holy shit.

His moves where tantalizing and surprisingly competent for someone never having done this before. Her legs began to shake with each pass around the sun he made and before she could control herself, she shattered above his mouth. He released his hold on her panties and grabbed both her ass cheeks while lapping her up, burying his face into her. His tongue was eager as he sucked and drank every single drop she gave. She bit her wrist to keep from screaming as he yanked down her thong and sat back upright. The skin of his dick was tight and dripped like a broken faucet, but before giving him what he was hoping for, she dropped to her knees and placed both hands on his. His chest heaved as he watched her tongue lick every inch of him. His head fell back and he slammed both of his hands against the walls beside him, almost breaking through the wood. He was close, and she knew it. She wanted to make this count for him, so spending too much time between his legs wouldn't end the way she wanted it to.

"I," he began but choked on his words before getting them out, "I need to feel what it's like to be inside of you. Please."

His voice was hypnotic and masculine. Plummeting her into an abyss of obedience and arousal. He grabbed her shoulders and pushed her away seconds before erupting into her mouth. She licked her lips as he leaned forward, grabbing her waist and pulling her onto his lap slowly. She straddled him and paced herself as she lowered down onto his bobbing cock. Teasing it with her entrance and allowing only a small bit of him inside her. He squeezed her ass so hard he nearly ripped her apart, but the pain only intensified her pleasure. It was desperate. Primal. Trying to lift his hips to get more of him inside of her, she continued to torture him. Spreading her juices over him, she sunk over his dick inch by inch in glorious agony. His fingers pulsed to the rhythm of her movements as he watched his shaft get swallowed whole inside of her. She coiled her fingers around his head and looked him dead in the eyes when he had reached full tilt. The penetration was indescribable and he almost exploded instantly, but she remained motionless so he could compose himself a little longer. She could feel his dick throb inside of her as she resumed her motions carefully by humping him instead of moving up and down. Grinding her clit against him and once again filling with urgent readiness. He kissed her. Passionately, and with a sense of gratitude she'd never felt before. When his tongue collided with hers, the walls inside of her clenched down on him causing him to grunt into her mouth. He couldn't help but pound his length in and out of her, holding her close and having her breasts rub against his chest.

He screamed into the air as years of abstinence came pouring out of him. She took all that he had to give as their bodies came together in a seemingly never-ending climax between two strangers. Covered in sweat, and riding out each of their orgasms, the pent up energy that ricocheted between them seemed never ending as he filled her with his cum. When the convulsions began to cease, they clung to each other, woven together in each other's arms. With him still inside of her, she laid her head on his broad shoulder as he massaged the tension from her back.

Panting, he spoke in his profoundly alluring deep voice, "You'll need to say the Act of Contrition and a boat load of Hail Mary's for what you've done."

She looked up at him in shock and he laughed.

"You don't say?"

"I do say," he bit her lower lip. "And, you have to do as I say, after all. If you seek penance that is."

"If penance means you between my legs, then yes, I do," She whispered seductively into his mouth.

"I'll give you penance," he kissed her. Softly. "After I plead for my own."

To be continued...

Chapter Nine

CONFESSION

PART TWO - ONE YEAR LATER

"Hello? Anyone home?" Trista yelled as she entered her mother's house.

"Hi, honey!" Her mom returned her greeting from somewhere upstairs. "Be down in a sec!"

After getting engaged to her boyfriend a few months ago, Trista's mom has transformed into a completely different person. Once lonely and unmotivated, she was now full of life and...happy. Something Trista hadn't seen in a while and she couldn't be happier for her. Tonight, her and Keith were throwing a dinner party so Trista could meet the rest of his family. Having exchanged a few texts with Keith's son after the little indiscretion the two had gotten themselves into, nothing ever came from it. And Trista was fine with that. Sleeping with a future 'family member' wasn't something high on her 'get it done' list. Having seen him a handful of times over the year, they were actually comfortable moving on and forgetting it ever happened. At least, so she thought.

"How many people are you expecting?" Trista yelled up the stairs after seeing the dining room table set for six.

"Turns out Keith's brother is going to join us, and of course Tim, as well as Aunt Jess," she answered while walking down the stairs.

"Oh cool," she loved hanging with her aunt more than she did most of her close friends. The woman had impeccable wit and next level confidence.

"Yeah," her mother fixed one place setting to make it perfect, and went for the kitchen. "I'm so excited for you to meet his brother. He's so neat."

"Neat?" Trista giggled. "That's an interesting adjective choice."

"You'll see," she smiled and the two of them prepped the rest of the food for the night.

The doorbell rang a half an hour later.

"I'll get it," Trista added the last bundle of washed grapes to the charcuterie board and went to get the door.

She could see three men through the glass, "The guys are here, Mom."

Opening the door while wiping a piece of cracker from her jeans, she lifted her head, and the color from her face dropped to her feet. No fucking way.

Keith's brother was a priest...and not just any priest. 'Her' priest. It had been quite some time since their taboo affair in the small confessional space and she had honestly tried for months to get him out of her mind. Having had a decent number of sexual experiences, nothing had quite satisfied her the way this holy man had. And now, standing face to face with him, and Keith's son Tim, made her feel a whole new level of indecent. He was wearing a white button down top, with the top two undone and fitted tan slacks. She swallowed hard and realized her gaze had dropped to his crotch. Prying her eyes from his visible bulge, her body rattled with sudden excitement.

Perfect.

"Hey, Trista," Keith leaned forward and kissed her on the cheek," she forced a smile as he walked past her and awkwardly nodded at the other two.

"How's it going?" Tim hugged her.

"It's going," she returned the greeting and turned toward Keith's brother. Her crotch remembered the way he made it feel. "I'm Trista, nice to meet you."

He took her hand, a very concerned expression on his face, and her stomach fluttered, "John."

Not wanting to expose the priest for his indiscretion, as well as her apparent promiscuity, she decided to pretend the two had never crossed paths before. And despite the initial nervous-as-fuck demeanor he had when the door first opened, he seemed pleased with her decision of disregarding their past. Although, she couldn't help but notice the stubble covering his face. He looked...defeated. She moved to her left and let them both in as her aunt skidded into the driveway, waving manically at her through the windshield. Trista giggled even though she was slowly dying inside. Jess was exactly what she'd need to make it through this night. Her, and a shit ton of Vodka.

Once everyone was inside and acquainted, Trista had yet to speak. Through the chatter of the meet and greets, Jess had convinced everyone that she feels it would be in the best interest of the female race to have John resign as a priest and join the world of the sinners. He was, of course, cordial and flattered, but the glances Trista's way portrayed a conflicted man. Trista couldn't help but feel the tangible tension between herself and him. Trying to soothe the onslaught of emotions trailblazing through her veins with Cosmos, she was finding herself entering a different realm of nonchalance. Which was not the best space to be in, considering the crowd. But she couldn't help it. Her heart rate was significantly elevated over normal levels and she knew she wouldn't be able to eat if she didn't relax her nerves somehow.

Adding insult to injury, Tim was, with no prompting what-so-ever, giving her the side-eye on occasion. Seriously? What the fuck? And of course, each time she looked over at him, he was looking back. Making the situation that much more horrible. The last thing she wanted was for Tim to think she'd be down to bone just because they had before, and that the alcohol was giving them a permission slip. Truth be told, she couldn't forget the sensations John's package had given her. Literally delivering her to heaven's gates. She downed the rest of her drink as dinner was ready to be served. As luck would have it, her mother had assigned the seats, placing Trista directly across from John. Feeling the heat of the booze suppress her inhibition, she sat feeling a certain degree of false confidence, and shame. The perfect combination for an intimate dinner.

So, just so I have it clear here, I've fucked my mother's fiancé's son and brother. Or should I say, Father? Yep, I'm that sort of slut.

"How's the new job, Trista?" Keith asked. Taking an oversized bite of meat and waiting for her answer.

"It's handled," she wrongly answered, immediately being aware of it and scrunching up her face.

"Nothing like being handled," Jess cheered, lifting her glass and toasting the air before taking a sip.

"Sorry," Trista shook her head. "It's going well. Thank you."

"What do you do for work?" Rev. John asked, looking particularly interested.

Don't talk to me. Literally, just take me to the bedroom.

"I'm the new admissions director over at Clark University," she sucked in her lips and grinned.

"Well that certainly is impressive," he nodded at her, causing her nipples to harden.

Son of a fucking bitch. He's a goddamned priest, Trista!

She looked over at Tim, praying he'd be more appealing to her. But nope, definitely didn't compare in the slightest. Not with the dramatic sensuality of the taboo situation combined with the inexperienced but highly attentive, and seemingly skilled, pleasure he had given to her. She wanted it again. Desperately.

Fuck, why did I think drinking would help? I'm legit going to be disowned.

After about an hour of eating and chatting, Trista was on her second glass of wine. Not only was she trying to remain calm despite the fact that John eye's had been burning her flesh since they sat down, she was happy to have a belly full of food to absorb some of the booze she'd consumed. She was definitely feeling relaxed. As well as extremely aroused. She crossed her legs to try and abate the nagging need between them, but she grazed the good Priest's pants with her bare toes in the process, adding to her devious excitement. He looked up at her, mid-sip, and paused his swallowing. Their eyes connected while the others discussed the latest town budget for road repair. He watched attentively as her chest heaved, and by the grace of God himself, his shoe made contact with her foot.

She swallow hard and grabbed her glass for another sip. Girl, stop drinking already!

John blinked away the trance he'd been caught in and excused himself from the table, "Which way to the washroom?"

"It's right through the kitchen," Trista's mother positioned her entire arm so it pointed to where the bathroom would be if there were no walls in the house.

"Thank you," he rose and grabbed a few plates on his way out.

"Thank you, John," her mother smiled at him as he passed.

"Of course," he couldn't have gotten out of there any faster.

Suddenly, Trista couldn't sit there surrounded by them anymore. Feeling embarrassed for making John so obviously uncomfortable, she decided to start the dishes while they continued their heated debate over the town's budget. The sounds of angry reasoning and debate filled the kitchen. Trista turned her head toward the direction of the bathroom and wondered what she'd do when he came out. Realizing she didn't want to be seen, she dried her hands and made her way toward the bathroom to sneak by it and down the hall to her old room. However, the moment she neared the corner, the door opened. She froze and they stared at each other, neither of them moving. A loud burst of laughter came from the dining room and they both turned their eyes toward it before returning their gazes to one another.

In that instant, he grabbed onto her shoulders and walked her backwards until she was against the hall wall. Keeping as quiet as humanly possible, he brought his face inches from hers while trying to steady his breathing. Her legs were jelly and if it weren't for being pinned, she'd have surely fallen over.

"I have a confession. I've thought about you every single day," he whispered, colliding his forehead with hers. Turning his face side to side he continued, "praying I'd have the strength to forget my sin. But the only thing it brought was an insatiable need to fantasize about you. Every spare second I have."

"I..." she tried to apologize.

"Shhh," he put a finger to her lips, pressing it against their softness and closing his eyes. "I can't think straight when it comes to you."

Same...

She opened her mouth and sucked in his finger. Twirling her tongue and tasting the salt on his skin. He watched and slowly brought his body to hers, pushing his growing erection between her legs.

"Trista?" Her Mother called. Their eyes bugged out and separated. "Could you turn the coffee on? It's ready to go."

"Sure thing!" She bolted over to the machine and flicked it on. As soon as she turned around, her eyes went to John's. He was leaning against the wall with the look of desire smeared across his face. She looked into the dining room and felt confident they were engrossed enough in their conversation. Their presence wouldn't be missed. Then she turned her face back toward John and walked toward him, but didn't stop. Looking him dead in the eyes as she passed, she walked right by him and down to her room. He watched as she disappeared from his view. Struggling between the growing need between his legs and the very real situation he was supposed to be a part of, his urges won. Keeping his hand on the wall, he followed her. Looking back only once before entering her room and closing her door.

She stood facing him, in front of her childhood bed covered in stuffed animals and frilly pillows and waited for his next move. Knowing they would have to be silent, the anticipation was hazardous. Remembering every single sound and movement he had made all those months ago, she could feel the moisture between her legs and the throbbing of her clit.

Yeah, being buzzed was definitely the right call. This is going to be fucking knock on Heaven's door hot. Sorry God, but you created him...not me.

"Not Your will, but mine be done," he mumbled as he approached her. "Let the wicked forsake his way."

She could barely hang on to what little rational thought she had left. Knowing he would soon be buried deep inside of her again wasn't something she was willing to talk herself out of. The words he spoke seeped into every crevice of her body and she knew right then and there that no matter how devoted he was to resist her, they would always be each other's weakness.

He stopped directly in front of her and reached forward to undo her jeans. Burning his eyes into hers, Trista remained still. The sound of her zipper lowering sent shocks of heat down her legs and up through her stomach and she had to reach behind her to grab onto the bed railing for support. He sensed the effect he had on her, which only tempted him more. Grabbing both sides of her jeans, he lowered them below her ass, exposing her white laced thongs. Falling to his knees, he continued to bring them down until they reached her ankles. Trista leaned to the side and freed herself from her pants, watching him watch her. When her legs were bare, she placed his hand against the place he longed to feel again.

"I've dreamed of this since the moment you walked out of the church, almost one year ago," his deep voice resonated through his body and onto her. She shivered in response and waited patiently for him to continue. Placing both of his hands against the front of her legs, he moved them around until they landed right below each of her ass cheeks, relishing the way her flesh felt beneath his palms. Allowing the weight of her ass to fall onto his fingers, he pushed her toward him until her scent reached his nose. He inhaled while rubbing his face against the front of her panties. "The kingdom of heaven is at my hands."

"Lock the door," she said pointedly and, without haste, did exactly as he was told. When he turned back to her, she had dropped her thong to the floor and used her finger to summon his return. He slammed both of his hands against his cheeks and pulled down his flesh at the sight. "Unfortunately, we don't have much time. The coffee takes about ten minutes to brew and time's almost up."

"I can't rush with you," he spoke with need and desperation as he approached her. Cupping her face in his hands, he studied her. "I want to know what your lips feel like against mine."

His words, along with the way he was so entranced by her, made her forget about what little time they had left. His thumbs circled her jaw before pushing it down, opening her mouth, and exposing her tongue. Keeping her arms down by her side, she was completely entranced by him. All she could hear was the sound of his breathing and the beating of her heart. Still, in his khakis, he pressed himself against her bare sex and watched her face react to the contact. He looked down between them and watched her nipples harden right before his eyes. Unable to wait any longer, he drew her firmly against him and grazed her bottom lip with his thumb.

She slithered her tongue out and teased this finger while looking up into his dark, brown eyes. This did him in. He lowered his head and froze before his mouth reached hers as if mentally preparing himself for what could quite possibly, ruin him forever. Feeling the heat radiating from between her legs and onto his trapped erection, there was no stopping him. At first, he simply grazed her lips with his, moving almost too slowly to see. A whimper escaped him as he continued to sample even the slightest touch. She could feel her clit pulse, begging to be next with each gentle passing he made across her mouth.

Knowing their time had most likely run out, a sense of urgency came over him. Slamming his mouth into hers, he lifted her off the floor and devoured all she was giving him. Their tongues became one in an unlockable kiss as he walked toward the bed. Lowering her down onto her back, not severing their lips, he supported her head and positioned himself directly on top of her. She wrapped her naked legs around him and melted underneath his gyrations. After a few moments, with their faces red, he pulled away and looked at her.

"Do you have any idea how beautiful you are?"

"Take off your pants," she demanded and toyingly bit his lower lip. He gave her a smirk fit for the devil and wasted no time unbuttoning, and lowering them to his knees before picking up where he left off.

The moment his body fell into place, he arched his back and lifted her shirt in order to expose her breasts. She wore a thin laced bra that her nipples protruded from and had to blink away the trance they immediately sent him into. Lowering enough to lick the tip of her left one, she squirmed under the weight of him.

"Careful," he warned, her wetness enticing him to fuck her.

"What's the matter?" she played coy and rubbed her clit back and forth against the head of his dick. "Do you want me to stop?"

"Absolutely not," he gave her nipple a gentle graze of his teeth before slithering down between her legs. "I simply need a taste from the fountain of pleasure. Since I'm already going to hell..."

"You're not going to..." she lost the ability to speak when his lips collided with her pussy. She could barely breathe through the aggression of his sucking. "Oh shit!"

She flung her hands over her mouth and tried to maintain silence despite the fact that she was being fucked by John's tongue. Switching between swirling around her swollen button and plunging deep into her walls, she was close to losing control and he knew it. There was no denying what the reactions she was showing meant, even to an inexperienced, yet gifted man.

"How are you so," she tried to speak but he resumed nursing her nerve with such power that it caused her legs to buck and wrap around his neck, "good at this!"

Pressing his tongue flat against her clit, he rubbed it while curving two of his fingers inside of her.

"Oh...fuck..." she grunted. Her legs violently shook and trapped his head within their spasm as he drew out her orgasm with ease. Flicking her G-spot until her body ceased and relaxed, he was now dripping all over the comforter and needed to let some of the tension go.

He unwrapped her legs and climbed up her body like a panther until the tip of his dick collided with her entrance. Giving him a wicked eye, she caught him off guard and promptly rolled him over onto his back, leaving her straddling him. The warmth of their sexes touching in the raw caused him to fling his arms around her and grab hold of her ass with the power of a God. Using his strength, he forced his cock through her plump lips, spreading her juices over him. She grabbed both of his arms and stretched them out to his sides, making a cross out of his body.

"Ready to get nailed?" She winked.

"You didn't just say that," he whispered.

She smirked and bent forward for another kiss. Sliding herself up and down his shaft, she humped him until she almost came. Between the caressing of his tongue inside her mouth and the pulsing she felt on his dick, she had to force herself to stop before it was too late. She wanted to come with him inside her, that much was certain. He couldn't handle her assault and forced his arms to come together in order to grab onto her ass once again. Lifting herself off of him, he squeezed her with readiness. She reached her hand down between their bodies and grabbed hold of his dick. He moaned beneath her cascading hair as she slowly lowered herself down onto it.

"Fuck," he breathed when the tip of his head was submerged inside of her.

"Shhh," she whispered, continuing to lower. Feeling him stretch her more than anything else ever had, her body began to tremble.

His hips moved ever-so-slightly to aid in the penetration and as he buried himself deeper and deeper, her mouth fell open in pleasure. He grunted and grit his teeth to prevent from exploding too soon but the minute she began bouncing on top of him, he knew it was only a matter of time. Figuring this wasn't the place to draw this out any further than it already had been, he slammed himself into her and pounded his cock through her tight walls. Gripping her waist, he used his arms to force her harder down onto him with each upward thrust.

Their fucking was fierce and uninhibited. She could feel the firm ridge of his head popping back and forth over her G-spot as she grinded her clit against his body, building her back up for round two.

"You feel so fucking incredible," she panted.

"I've been waiting for you," he pushed himself deep inside her, "all this time."

She fell onto him and he wrapped his arms around her as they brought each other to the edge. Hearing the suction through their sex, he lifted his knees to allow himself more momentum in his thrusts. Reaching for his mouth, Trista locked their lips once again and they both mimicked their fucking with their tongues. Within seconds their bodies spiraled into unimaginable pleasure.

"Oh fuck," he snarled his words against her teeth as his orgasm completely took over him, leaving him pouring years worth of cum into her.

With each spasm his dick made, she rode them until her release erupted throughout her body. Ricocheting from deep inside her belly and throughout each of her nerves. He held her close and together they trembled in each other's embrace for what felt like hours. When the fibers inside of them started to dwindle in their frenzy, she collapsed on top of him. Laying silent apart from their panting, they both were drunk on the euphoria that had just run through them.

"Trista?" Her mother's voice called from down the hall.

"Oh shit!" Trista whispered and popped herself off of him. "Quick, I have an idea."

Feeling a little dizzy on her feet, she clumsily retrieved her jeans and flung them on while he did the same. She hurried over to the window and slid it open.

"You first," she smiled, her face eight shades of pink.

"What then?"

"Just do what I do," she silently clapped him into action and within seconds they were both outside. "Follow me."

They walked to the front door and back into the house as if nothing had happened.

"See, I told you the tree was dead. Pay up," she mused.

"Where were you two?" Jess asked with a look of pure curiosity.

"When John came out of the bathroom he asked me about the creepy maple tree out back. I told him it was dead and he bet me it wasn't. So, we went out the back to inspect the ghastly arbor." Trista was very proud of her cover up, despite the sudden intense need to sit.

"I wasn't aware you were such a tree inquisitor," Keith joined in.

"It's a recent development," John reached into his back pocket to pay her. Only his wallet wasn't there. He shot Trista a look and she chuckled.

"Welp, here's to new interests," Tim toasted, winking at Trista.

Oh God...sorry junior. I've got something much more divine, and I'm not about to let him go.

To be continued...

CHAPTER TEN

LIBERATION

PART THREE - TWO MONTHS LATER

J ohn looked deep into his own eyes while adjusting his clerical collar in a mirror hanging by the door of his vestry. His four o'clock mass was about to begin and he needed to clear his mind of her. Again. Becoming ritual, he was finding it progressively more difficult to rid his thoughts of the way her body felt against his. Falling deeper into the entrapment of his primitive make-up, John struggled with his oath to the church. Telling Trista shortly after their family gathering that he had made a commitment and needed to see it through. She hadn't said much, but the look on her face still haunts him. Knowing the decision, he made to end things and try to repent for his concupiscent indiscretions was the right one, John struggled to make it through each day with the weight of his sins on his shoulders along with the relentless entrapment she had on his being. It was bad enough he'd often find himself needing to drive by her childhood home where their bodies had connected last, knowing full well that that sort of behavior could easily be deemed as obsessive. But he took comfort in knowing that, during a weak moment when he had dug deep in order to find her current living address, he had yet to bring himself to go.

Every hour consisted of him performing robotically in front of anyone that crossed his path and for the hundreds of devote parishioners that depended on him to bring them closer to God. Delivering the word of Christ in a cathartic manner in order to ensure their feelings of connectedness to the Lord, John often prayed the hymns he preached would penetrate his guilt and alleviate him of his own torment. Although it's already been months and everything John sees, reminds him of the way Trista moved when he touched her. Unable to thwart the need to touch himself, John found the only way to sleep most nights was to envision Trista forcing herself onto him. As if somehow that made it all okay. It was either that, or live with the pain abstinence would surely deliver unto him. Making a fist and shaking it back open, John put on his face and exited his room.

...

Trista needed a minute. Or several thousand. Between the awkward exchanges she had with Tim at every corner and the fact that he still very much wanted to continue their secret affair as if he was living out a real life porno made her unsure of where her life was taking her. And of course, not to forget the formidable realization that she'd never feel John's fingers run down her stomach again or the way he made her feel like she was the most desirable thing he'd ever laid eyes on. And it was true, Tim was showing some hard-core interest, but after being with John, she struggled to find anyone else who could even hold a flame the way he did. Even with his limited experience, Trista, still, often relived the commanding arousal his hands had given to her the last time they were together. Trying to forget the night they had met up and he let her know that he could no longer do this, she spent most of her time fantasizing about him changing his mind and kicking the door down in order to get to her.

Wanting to send him a text more than she needed water to live, Trista knew their affair was not ordinary and sympathized when she witnessed the visible agony on his face. Tempted to reach out and make him forget all about his oaths and promises, her respect for him allowed her to let him go. But it did not remove him from her dreams. Drinking more than she used to in the hopes of forgetting all about him, she needed to muster the enthusiasm her mother required of her so the two could plan the most successful wedding this side of the Mississippi.

Buried in plans and magazine rip-outs, Trista couldn't help but daydream about the big event. Knowing exactly who'd be marrying them, along with the location being in the most romantic places on Earth, Trista packed her most alluring bikinis and outfits. Feeling a twinge of second-guessing her wardrobe and teasing him, she only hoped he hadn't completely forgotten about her. For all she knew, he had a life-long itch he needed to scratch in order to carry out the rest of his days being celibate. And she was simply at the right place and at the right time. But even the most uncertain parts of her subconscious knew that the way he took his time and devoured each and every inch of her wasn't the act of simple curiosity. He single-handedly transported her to unearthly levels of ecstasy by reaching deep enough inside of her that he was able to grab hold of her carnal sensuality and coax it to the surface. Where it has remained neglected. A dangerous splinter she continuously tried to remove by drowning it out with booze.

Looking around her second-floor apartment for anything else she may need for the trip, Trista tossed the book she just bought called ALL THINGS THAILAND and tossed it into her purse. Grabbing her luggage and overnight bag, she was ready to go and overly ready to see John. The recurring dreams of him sneaking out of his hotel room to come and find her made it hard for her to think about anything else.

The driver honked his horn and she made her way down to the street. Her mother was already in the car waiting with a smile as wide as the Nile River, which made Trista happy. It's not often you find love again later in life and Trista only hoped she'd have a chance at even a first go of it before she turned thirty.

Taking the bags from her arms, the suited man placed her things in the trunk and then opened the back door for her to get in.

"It's finally here!" Trista shrieked excitedly while entering the car next to her mother.

"I can't believe it's happening," her eyes were glossed over.

"It's going to be epic, Mom," Trista buckled up and they made their way.

"The boys all landed earlier this morning and I got a text from Keith saying the resort is unbelievable and that he couldn't wait for me to be added to its beauty." She was choked up and Trista could feel her mother's elation.

"Wow," Trista grabbed her phone to look at the text, "that's the most romantic thing I've ever heard."

"You know," she winked at Trista, "too bad Tim will be your step-brother. I think he's got an innocent crush on you."

"Wow, Mom," he gave her back her phone, "let's pretend you didn't just say that."

The ride was quick and the flight was long as hell, but after almost a lifetime of travel, the two women left the airport and hopped into the cab that would take them each to the men they longed to see.

...

"They're in the cab and on their way," Keith told Tim and John.

"Cheers my brother," John rose his beer off the outside resort bar top and clanked it with his and Tim's. "To a lifetime of happiness."

"Thanks, bro," Keith's cheeks were red as he looked down at his drink bubbling after taking a gulp. "Saying I lucked out would be a drastic understatement. The woman was quite literally created to match every single part of me."

"Did you put that in the vows, Dad?" Tim jabbed him in the arm. They all chuckled and took another sip while taking in the scenery.

The most vibrant colors overwhelmed every corner their eyes traveled, starting from the magic hue of the water to the massive rock formations reaching up to the sky. Blankets of green hid the multitude of wildlife from onlookers but allowed them the safe refuge to spy on whatever they felt like with curiosity. It was truly the second most gorgeous sight John had ever laid his eyes on, which immediately time-warped him back to her thighs, and his hand running up the inside of them. It was the softest, most reactive skin he'd ever felt and the cause of all his affliction. A strong gust of floral soaked wind passed over him, and he inhaled the aroma while images of Trista's glistening pussy played in his mind as if she was lying spread-open right in front of him.

"John?" Keith tapped his brother's back.

"Oh, sorry," John turned back toward the table and chugged the rest of his beer. Both Tim and Keith watched in shocked amusement. "Got caught in a daze. Must be jet lagged some."

"Well since you just pounded your beer," Keith placed his hand on John's shoulder, "feel free to take a time out. I'll wake you for dinner."

"Sounds perfect," John shoveled out some cash to cover the whole tab and tossed it on the table.

"No, man," Keith started but when John flashed him a look that could not be mistaken, Keith nodded. Being only two years apart, John was considerably more dominant than Keith, who exuded a milder and more accommodating demeanor. "Thanks, John. See you in a bit."

'Good deal," John walked through the touristy lobby. Completely overrun with new check-ins and the verbal chaos of cheer and awe, he meandered his way through the thick cluster to get to the elevator on the opposite side.

Couples kissing and making goo-goo eyes at each other dominated the collection and John tried to keep his diminishing wits about him. Rattled to his core as to what was to come, even the thought of seeing Trista again threatened his ability to remain decent in public. Knowing he shouldn't have let his mind run wild with images of her, the longer the time stretched since their last time together seemed to bring him closer to the darkest part of his insanity. A place where his lust patiently waits, as if knowing something he doesn't yet.

Colliding with a female about three-quarters his size, John swiftly crouched down to help retrieve the contents of her purse.

"I'm so sorry," she giggled, not seeming to care her most intimate possessions rolled free under the feet of strangers.

"No need," he reached to grab the last tampon and almost fell on all fours when he realized the pair of feet it had rested against. Allowing his eyes to direct his head, he slowly stood until he was towering over her. "Trista."

"John!" Trista's mother shrieked and jumped into his stunned arms. Trying to put on an acceptable greeting, John kept his eyes on hers while lowering her mother back to her feet. "Where is Keith?"

"He and Tim are out that way toward the bar," he couldn't take his eyes off of Trista, who also struggled with the same affliction.

His heart hammered in his chest and if it weren't for the fans overhead, he may have passed out. She was wearing a light-blue spaghetti-strapped dress that flowed in the breeze, exposing her perfect legs. And no matter how hard he tried, he couldn't stop himself from stealing glances of her neck, covered by the few strands of hair that had escaped her clip in the breeze. His eyes took in every inch of her soft skin as they ventured lower to her breasts, which heaved up and down as she watched him examine her.

"Trista," her mom's voice echoed inside his head as if it had come from a dream. "Would you mind waiting in line so I can go see Keith?"

"Of course," Trista cleared her throat, and off she went, disappearing in the crowd. Looking back at John, who was visibly distressed, she softly spoke, "there you are."

He couldn't swallow. Being ever conscious of restraining himself from grabbing her and inhaling the scent coming from the nape of her neck, John's right eyebrow faintly bounced as a smile forced its way onto his face.

...

Trista couldn't believe how sexy she found the man standing in front of her. Still, after all this time. The instant he threw himself to the floor to help her mother, she knew it was him. She could smell it. And when he went for that Kotex, she nearly moaned out loud at the thought of him touching her exposed toes. Missing the feral nature his inexperienced hands brought to her was indescribable and utterly addicting. No matter how many variations of vibrators, imaginary images of him between her legs was a craving that had remained present since they were last together almost a year ago. However, she knew that no matter how long she'd have to wait, she'd never forget the way he absorbed every move, every kiss, and every tremble she made.

"Trista!" Tim's voice shot through the chaos and smacked both of them in the face. "You're already checked in! Come get a drink!"

She spotted him about forty people width away and waved back before looking back at John, who still had yet to speak, "Should we join the others?"

"I'm afraid I'll have to pass this time," his eyes burrowed into her, "I need...rest. I'll see you at dinner."

He softened his features and nodded respectfully at her before disappearing within the human camouflage. Trista was left standing alone, wishing she could follow him and see if he'd be willing to rub some sunscreen on her back. Or fuck her. Either would do and certainly wouldn't be picky. She found it funny, not funny haha but more along the lines of 'why the fuck do we do this to ourselves?', respecting someone's wishes to the point that you have to suffer as a consequence. But when she first met John, she was in a less-than-ideal state of mind and she wanted to be a decent person, which meant to not tempt a priest with her wayward behavior. She figured maybe then he'd see her in a new light and have no other choice than to succumb to her mature charms, which she was well aware defeated the entire purpose.

Deciding to be better than the person inside of her taunting her with sensations fabricated by her libido, she inhaled her surrender and walked toward Tim to join the others outside. It wasn't entirely the worst thing being here, as she was pleasantly distracted by the jungle meets ocean feel and the wide variety of birds singing all around them. It was truly an ambiance one could easily get swept away in if not careful. And despite the telling looks Tim was already throwing her way, it would take a lot more than the Gulf of Thailand and all its wonders to change her mind on that front. The fact of the matter was, Trista would need a distraction if she was going to be able to thwart her burning desire for John, and as luck would have it, a very visible fruity-based cocktail swaying in her mother's hand was just the thing to numb out the pain of having to go without the greatest sex of her life.

The sun was setting slower than molasses rolling down a wooden spoon and Trista wasn't mad about it. Almost three drinks in, the music had taken hold of her body as she tried to coax her mother to dance with her.

"I'm beat, babe," she grabbed hold of both Trista's shoulders, "I don't even think I can make it through dinner. Rain check?"

"Alright Mama," Trista kissed her on the forehead. "Sleep tight you two. And remember...no sneaking a peek, Keith! Stay in your room!"

"Yes ma'am," he saluted her and took hold of his bride-to-be's arm. Leaving Trista alone with Tim.

"Party poopers," Tim winked and sipped down the rest of his drink. "You hungry?"

"I could eat," she definitely needed to eat. Her surroundings hadn't yet started to spin, but she was close to that and needed something to soak up some of her 'pour' choices.

Luckily, the restaurant was only a few yards from the bar and as they walked in awkward silence, images of John slithered through her mind. She couldn't help but feel like now would be a great time for him to show up and whisk her away to some outdoor secret spot and have his way with her. The thought alone turned her on and the only guy insight that seemed interested in her was not something she'd ever revisit. She supposed she'd have to break the news to him, and figured tonight would be the perfect time. Spare them the weirdness that would follow them for the rest of the trip otherwise. John was already too close to home as it was, and Tim was an even more ridiculous option. She was beginning to think she had serious issues and wondered if her wayward behavior could have been influenced by the endless reruns of All In the Family she'd watched while growing up.

After telling the hostess it was only going to be the two of them, they lucked out and got a table along the edge of the dining area that overlooked the ocean. Trista was actually grateful her mom ducked out early, because now more than ever she wanted to end Tim's hopefulness of a lifelong secret affair. With John, however, she'd be willing to do just about anything. Somehow, to her, he was worth all the risk and heartache that would most likely come of it.

"Well, this doesn't suck," Tim leaned forward while dragging in his chair and looking around.

"It's quite the place," she took a long sip of her water. When the server approached them, she knew exactly what she wanted to order after seeing it on the table next to them.

"Hello," a petite Thai woman dressed in a fitted white pantsuit greeted them. "Welcome to Thailand. Can I get you two love birds a drink?"

Trista coughed, "I'll stick with the water for now, thank you."

"I'll have a vodka cranberry, please," Tim flashed a mega-watt smile at her, which didn't go unnoticed. She immediately loosened up and lost all previous poise. She turned to leave and got their order started.

"She's adorable," Trista mentioned, hoping to veer his attention elsewhere.

"Isn't she?" He spoke the words but was looking right at Trista.

"Look, Tim," Trista began but stopped when he placed his hands over hers on top of the table.

Trista tried to pull the away but he held firm, "No, don't say it."

"Get. Your. Hands. Off. Of. Her," his voice vibrated through her back and right into Tim.

Trista face softened at the sound and every cell within her tingled causing her skin to break out in goosebumps.

John...

...

He tried to stay calm while walking through the restaurant to get to them. Knowing he was late for their dinner, he immediately spotted Trista across the entire room and practically barreled over the hostess to get to her when he saw Tim reach for what was his. He'd never experienced that level of anger and could hardly breathe past the sensation of fear that he had lost her. Knowing that was what he had initially needed, he was faced with the strong realization that ultimately it was her he wanted to devote his life to, not God. The forces inside of him proved too powerful to combat and while he showered in his hotel room, he came to the conclusion that this was what he wanted. However, seeing another man touching her sent him into such a state of possession, he knew the inexperience he had with such emotions could prove disastrous if he didn't proceed carefully.

"John?" Tim released her hands and gave his uncle a confused look. "I didn't think you'd be joining us."

John couldn't speak and all he could hear was the rush of blood pounding through his ear drums.

"You alright, man?" Tim looked concerned and Trista slowly turned her head back to face John.

Her face gave away all her feelings for him as the intensity in his eyes burned through her. "I need you...to come with me."

"What?" Tim interjected.

"Now," he was breathless.

Trista stood, knowing nothing on this planet could prevent her.

"What's going on?" Tim demanded.

"Tim," Trista began but John tangled his fingers around hers and pulled her away from the table. Leaving Tim utterly confused and embarrassed. Without speaking, she blindly followed him, his musky scent sweeping over her face and promising nothing but the two of them caught up in the rapture their bodies created together.

Walking through the dark paths that weaved and coiled like a labyrinth within the trees of the resort, John led them to an inlet carved into stone along the shore. Dressed with pillows and candles, Trista stood in awe at the romanticized feel of it.

Before entering their hidden alcove, John stopped walking and turned to her, "Trista," he inhaled to try and pause his shaking. She grabbed his wrists and looked into his eyes. "You've managed to infiltrate my entire being. Completely encapsulating everything my life's mission had once been about. Which was to find peace, and spread it to others. You've taken me to places I never thought I'd ever visit. I am a hard man to get through to, However, the effect your voice had on me the very first time I heard you speak seems to have changed my DNA somehow. I find myself with a longing that only calms when being with you."

"John," Trista couldn't believe her ears and knew right then and there that he'd be the only one capable of taking her breath away, "I've been yours since the moment you opened the door to my chamber."

He clenched his teeth and she could see his muscles flex around his jaw as she loosened her grip on him and gently coiled her fingers over the tops of his hands. Closing his eyes in order to take in all the sensations the simple gesture delivered to him, he turned his hands around and allowed her wrists to fall into his palms before walking backward toward the hidden retreat.

Her dress flowed wild in the ocean breeze as she climbed onto the mattress first, exposing her ass to him. Unable to control himself, he placed both hands on either side of her hips and circled them while manipulating her cheeks to move as he wished. Trista's eyes closed and she nearly fell forward from the onslaught of arousal his touch gave her. Climbing in behind her, he lifted her so she was kneeling between his knees, holding her back against his chest. Trista let her head fall back against his shoulder as his face brushed up and down the side of her neck, taking her to a place of pure euphoria. His hands pressed hard against her quads and moved upward to her stomach, avoiding her most deprived place as his growing need for her dug into her backside.

Feeling every inch of her, John let every thought, every doubt, and every reservation in his mind evaporate until the only thing present was her connection to him. Nothing in this world could compare to the feeling he experienced touching her. Devouring her neck, he let his hands remember the way she felt in their command and he was convinced nothing could possibly pull him away. He was addicted. Savoring every sound she made, he knew he'd have to take things slow when the crevice of her ass cradled his growing cock. Still clothed in his thin linen pants, it was easy to feel her heat press down on him.

She lifted her arms and wrapped them behind his head, exposing her chest for him to caress. Which he did not let go to waste. With his thumbs outstretched, he cupped each of her breasts in his hands underneath her dress. Moaning, they both fell captive to the length of time they'd waited for this moment and the realization that they'd have the freedom to be together. Startling him, Trista turned around and wrapped herself around his body. Squeezing her legs around his back and gripping the hair on the back of his head, they looked into each other's eyes and revealed the unspoken words of their need for one another. Without warning, John dropped his head and pressed his forehead into her chest. A non-sexual act that he could only attribute to him finally accepting the decision he made to change his path.

When she started to move on top of him, he dug his fingers into her back, massaging her while manipulating her gyrations against his cock. Their breathing echoed around them on the rock chamber as the ocean waves crashed behind them. With not a person in sight, they were left free to explore each other without the worry of being seen. The resort surely knew what they were doing when constructing these little pods of paradise. Despite both of them being fully clothed, John knew what he needed. And that wasn't to simply drive himself inside of her as if she was a conquest but to relish all that she was and all that she did to him. He planned on making this his new life mission. He'd deal with the consequences later.

Now fully erect and wedged between her ass cheeks, John kept a rhythm that stimulated each of them. He could very well finish right here and now, considering the length of time he'd kept himself in a state of torture to repent for his sins, but the pain of holding out was far too tempting. And he was all about temptation now that the cloth had been dropped. The way she responded to every ounce of pressure he dug into her, and every breath he released atop her skin, transported him to a place he had longed for his entire life. It seemed, to him, that each time he'd been with her only increased his hunger for her. He was convinced this was what every human soul searched for, and now that he had found it, there was no way he'd ever give it up. He was enthralled and truly fascinated by this woman and knowing his potential to remain devoted, despite his recent weakness for the flesh, nothing would ever change that.

Her movements against his shaft were intentional, not incessant or forced, but gradual and patient, and with each forward motion she made, her nipples trailed up his chest. Fed up with the material between them, John grabbed her dress and flung it over her head and tossed it away. More than pleased to see that she was bare-breasted, he curled his fingers into her thong and ripped them apart, causing her an ounce of fire-fueled pain. Now, completely naked and on top of him, he buried his face into her neck and massaged every inch of her backside while she continued to rub herself against him.

"Trista," he breathed into her nape while flexing his hips upward into her.

"Let me take care of you," she whispered into his ear and slithered down his body until her face was inches from his bulge.

John watched her intently as she slowly undid his button and lowered the zipper. Sliding her hand into the opening, he panted when her hand found his dick ready to spring free from the confines of his boxers. Having limited exposure to having his dick sucked, the only other time being by her briefly in the confessional, he watched intently as her body slithered like a panther as she toyed with him as if she was curious. Which he both appreciated and cursed. Rubbing her cheek against the length of him while carefully kneading his balls with both of her hands, John's mouth hung open as he gripped her hair.

Wanting nothing more than to feel her warm lips wrapped tightly around him, he could tell she wasn't about to give in to his desires that easily. Fighting the urge to close his eyes, he kept his focus on the junction between her ass as it curved up behind her. Keeping her mouth barely off of his tip, allowing the moisture from her breath to dampen him, John's entire body trembled with need. And as if she was aware of this, he noticed a smile grace her beautiful face.

"If God were to deem it my time to go for the sins of my body, I'd go happily after being with you," his words hummed into her and with that she allowed her mouth to take him in. He grunted and almost exploded immediately when her silky tongue ran down the bottom side of his dick, "Holy Mary, Jesus, and Joseph."

Lifting her head back to the top of him, she circled her tongue around his tip and flicked the base of it until he was twitching on his knees. Squeezing her hair harder, the restraint needed to not fuck her face was strong as he allowed the sensations to consume him. Sucking him in, he jolted his legs together and flung her off of him.

"Sorry," he quivered. "I don't want to come like that. Not this time."

She leaned forward on all fours and crawled over him until their faces were a hairline apart. Licking her lips, John grabbed her face in both of his hands and fell back, bringing her with him. Laying on top of his clothed body, he rolled them over so he could take back his control. Rock hard and dripping, he stood, leaving her on the bedding looking up at him. She watched with seductive eyes as he lowered his pants and unbuttoned his shirt. She teased him by opening her legs and snaking her hand over her pussy. Forgetting to remove his top, he stood paralyzed as she swirled her finger over her nerve while looking directly into his eyes.

"The power you hold over me is mighty," he spoke robotically. "Have mercy on my soul."

Dropping to his knees, he took her playing hand into his and brought her finger to his mouth and licked it before taking one of her legs and placing it onto his shoulder. Falling back onto her elbows, she watched as he lowered enough that half of his face was hidden by her sex. Seeing only his eyes and the top of his nose, he flicked her moistened clit until her body started to shake. Unable to wait any longer to taste her, his mouth collided with the sweetest thing he'd ever tasted. Forcing his tongue deep inside of her, he gripped her ass with both hands and forced her against him. Using his strength, he slid her up and down the entirety of his mouth while his upper lip massaged her pulsing nerve.

"Come for me," he whispered into her. "Please give me your release."

His words shattered her and she flung her other leg around his back, convulsing and trapping him in their grasp. He moaned into her as he spread her wetness around her opening for an easier entrance, knowing how small she was compared to him. When her body stilled, she grabbed his hair and pulled him up until he was laying directly on top of her. His cock dangled between her soaked legs and when she scratched her nails up and along the sides of him and under his shirt, he let his weight rest on her so he could kiss the need off of her face.

Allowing her to taste herself on him, they let their tongues dance in the privacy of their locked lips as he pressed the head of his dick into her entrance. She let out a scream and could no longer maintain their oral play as he watched her face change with each inch he buried within her. Cradling her head in his hand, he used his other to grab under her lower back, arching her ever so slightly as he continued to get lost inside her tight walls. Going as slow as he could to avoid exploding too soon, he resumed kissing her.

She squeezed around him and purred in his mouth, "take me."

"Shhhh," he warned, "be still."

"I can't," she gyrated under him as he remained still. "I need you."

"Trista," he could barely get the words out, "please. Let me."

He was relieved when she listened and to reward her while he regained his control, he began pumping her while pressing firmly against her re-growing nerve.

"Oh, John," she panted. "Faster."

"I...can't," he was struggling and he was close to throwing in the towel and just having at her. Knowing there would be many many more times to have prolonged sessions.

"If you keep doing this," she grunted when he pushed deep into her, "I'm going to come again."

Listening, he continued. Her walls began to twitch around the thickness of his shaft and without further restraint, he was done for.

"I'll be damned, fuck it," he pounded into her and within seconds her slick tunnel collapsed around him and her screams got lost in the thunderous sounds of the ocean. His balls coiled, shooting heat through his cock until he exploded inside of her. Roaring in ecstasy, he hammered his orgasm out by fucking her harder than he knew was even possible, pouring all of his pent-up celibacy into her. Meeting him thrust for thrust, their release continued without end. Pleasure ricocheted through them both as they tried to grip onto each other as hard as they could for stability.

After what seemed an eternity of bliss, John looked down at her red-soaked face and sweat-covered body. Moving his gaze down to her breasts and leaning down to kiss each of her hardened nipples, she giggled and hugged him close.

"Does this mean I have to wait another year before I get to have you again?" She panted.

"Absolutely not," he was breathless. "I was thinking tomorrow, same time, same place."

"Nothing in this world could stop me from showing up," she looked deep into his eyes when he lifted his head.

"I was hoping you'd say that," he kissed her passionately for some time. When they came up for air, she had a wicked look on her face. "What is it?"

"Can I get an amen?" She burst into laughter.

"Really?" he acted unamused.

"I had to," she bit his lower lip.

"Yeah," he sighed. "I have a feeling the cracks won't stop with you."

"You can bet the Bible on that."

He shook his head and they kissed until dawn. Having at least three more rounds of fucking before the sun rose. Truly living like Adam and Eve without a care in the world now that they had one another. And their affection quickly grew into love, which defined the rest of their days.

THE END

THANK YOU FOR READING MY LITTLE TALES!

I hope they tickled your fancy and twisted your sheets.

Keep your eyes peeled for volume two coming **SUMMER OF 2024** and will include the favorites:

Alive, My Cherished, Hunted, Fluid, Warranty, and The Prisoner

And four new stories:

Wet, Het Stroking, Hallowed Be Thy Neighbor, and Tonight

AND MANY, MANY THANKS TO MY MASTER BETAS:

Your feedback was invaluable to me and I have enjoyed bantering with you over your favorite scenes!

Chelsey Aniece

Daphnee Blaquiere

Lacey Rider

Nikki Pellichero

Theresa Styles

Whitney Lafrenz

Danny Waldo

Ellen Coley

Jean

Marie

Hali Linville

Gabriella Marie

Jennifer R Hale

Cami

BookishJenn

Mariah Baker

Loz Books

Sophie Newell

Sauieh

Laura K

A.Keys

Bee

Cass Bella

Michelle Bigley

LauRen

Jose Manuel Albarracin

Jherrica Coleman

BigTittieGothGirl

Sunshine

Kaylyn Wilkerson

Tanya Harriott

Shannon Emerick

Kimmy Diaz

Danny Waldo

Hali Linville

Candis Lashley

Nicole Pellichero

Ben Roberts

Dayana D Eusebio C

Bee Snyder

Elaine Brown

MDMD

Bee Snyder

Natalí S.B.

Becca O'keefe

Shanell Thomas

Sophie Newell

Laura Kavolius

Kaylyn Wilkerson

Chauntel Nicole

Sienna Austin-Monroe

Booked_Bybec

Have You Read Reviews

Kimberly Leong

Becca O'Keefe

Jade Blue

Aly Pixie Demon

Andrea Marlow

Elizabeth Rasmuson

Kelly Van Doorn

Becca Flannigan

Kate P.L.

Milton Keynes UK
Ingram Content Group UK Ltd.
UKHW051931050124
435541UK00002B/35